SERPENT ROSE

NewCon Press Novellas

Set 1: Science Fiction (Cover art by Chris Moore)
The Iron Tactician – Alastair Reynolds
At the Speed of Light – Simon Morden
The Enclave – Anne Charnock
The Memoirist – Neil Williamson

Set 2: Dark Thrillers (Cover art by Vincent Sammy)
Sherlock Holmes: Case of the Bedevilled Poet – Simon Clark
Cottingley – Alison Littlewood
The Body in the Woods – Sarah Lotz
The Wind – Jay Caselberg

Set 3: The Martian Quartet (Cover art by Jim Burns)
The Martian Job – Jaine Fenn
Sherlock Holmes: The Martian Simulacra – Eric Brown
Phosphorous: A Winterstrike Story – Liz Williams
The Greatest Story Ever Told – Una McCormack

Set 4: Strange Tales (Cover art by Ben Baldwin)
Ghost Frequencies – Gary Gibson
The Lake Boy – Adam Roberts
Matryoshka – Ricardo Pinto
The Land of Somewhere Safe – Hal Duncan

Set 5: The Alien Among Us (Cover art by Peter Hollinghurst)
Nomads – Dave Hutchinson
Morpho – Philip Palmer
The Man Who Would be Kling – Adam Roberts
Macsen Against the Jugger – Simon Morden

Set 6: Blood and Blade (Cover art by Duncan Kay)
The Bone Shaker – Edward Cox
A Hazardous Engagement – Gaie Sebold
Serpent Rose – Kari Sperring
Chivalry – Gavin Smith

SERPENT ROSE

Kari Sperring

NewCon Press
England

First published in the UK by NewCon Press
41 Wheatsheaf Road, Alconbury Weston, Cambs, PE28 4LF
August 2019

NCP 200 (limited edition hardback)
NCP 201 (softback)

10 9 8 7 6 5 4 3 2 1

ISBN:

978-1-912950-25-6 (hardback)
978-1-912950-26-3 (softback)

Cover art and internal illustration by Duncan Kay
Cover layout by Ian Whates

Minor Editorial meddling by Ian Whates
Book layout by Storm Constantine

Author's Dedication:

For Moira J Shearman, always.
朋友的眼睛是最好的镜子
The best mirror is a friend's eyes.

One

"Again!" Lamorak rolls to his feet, brushing straw from his shoulders, and looking hopeful. He's sixteen years old and fairly new to court. For all that, he's quick to learn how to get his way. I've seen the same look on greedy spaniels.

"No."

"Oh, come on."

"No, Lamorak. I've got other things to do. Go and ask Kay: he's master-at-arms."

"I don't want to ask Kay. Kay doesn't *like* me."

"Ask one of your brothers, then. One of *my* brothers? One of Sagremore's brothers?"

"You're making fun of me! Gaheris, you're my only friend."

"No, I'm not. You have plenty of friends."

"The only person who has time for me, then. Gaheris, *please.*"

"No. Go and ask Aglovale."

"I don't want Aglovale. I want you. You're far more…"

"… Stupid?"

"Sympathetic."

"Oh, that's a new one. I like that. Gaheris is sympathetic. Spelt g-u-l-l-i-b-l-e." I pick up my jerkin from the newel post and start to put it on. "No, Lamorak."

He has snake's eyes, long and cunning and yellow. They watch me reproachfully for a moment, then he turns his back. "It doesn't

7

matter, anyway." He goes to the door, rests his head on the frame. "Forget it."

He sounds as though he's thinking of crying. That's another move I've learnt to recognise. I hesitate, with one boot on. "Lamorak, listen. I have duties to attend to, and you should be in the tilting yard practising knightly ways, not up here learning to wrestle."

He doesn't look round. He's not to be assuaged so easily. "Kay's in charge of training, and Kay doesn't like me."

"So? It's hardly personal. Kay doesn't like anybody. He told me yesterday that I was the most uncoordinated fighter he'd met this side of a duck. And I've been knighted ten years. It's just his way."

"But he makes me feel so worthless."

"Well, ignore it. You're already far better than I was at your age. He's just trying to make sure you keep working."

He turns, tears gone. "D'you really think so?"

"Yes. Kay…"

"No, about me. Am I really any good?"

His moods are ridiculous. Like talking to a woman. Smiling, I finish putting my boots on, and say "Yes, I think you're very good."

"For my age?"

"Don't fish." Lamorak looks plaintive. "Saint Anne! No, not just for your age. In comparison with all of us. Oh, you're not up to Lancelot, or my brother Gareth, but… You're certainly as good as I am – better, probably, though that's hardly difficult – you'd give Bors a run for his money, or Dinadan… "I tail off. "You're fine."

I'm very slow, sometimes. Lamorak's eyes light up, and he blocks my exit, grinning. "Then I hardly need Kay's training, do I? So we…"

Like all that family, he's built slight and wiry. It's easy enough to turn him, with a hand on his shoulder. "Who's that, with the blue cockade?'

"Sir Gareth. But…"

"But nothing. Gareth's out there, working with Kay. And if he needs it, you do. Yes?"

"Yes… But surely you… "He looks up over his shoulder at me.

"*I have to go.*" I can stare him down, sometimes… After a minute, he shrugs, and swings out onto the ladder. He's only made me an hour late. I wait for him to reach the bottom before stepping out myself. With my weight, there's no point in taking risks. Halfway to the stable gate, he pauses, and looks round at me.

"Gaheris?"

"Umm?"

"Am I really better than you?"

"What a great achievement! Yes, I expect so." He's frowning, as though that troubles him. "What of it?"

"You always do that… "I want to start walking again, but he puts out a hand to stop me. "Will you fight with me, then? Swords?"

"Not now."

"No, but…"

"You won't learn anything. Better to ask Aglovale."

"Gaheris?" He sounds, I don't know, somehow anxious. His hand is on my arm, shaking it like a child. "Please?"

I sigh. What can one do? "All right. Swords." He takes the hand away, bouncing. "But, Lamorak…"

"Yes?"

"*Tomorrow.*"

There are four of us in all: four tall northern sons of Lot, tolerated in this southern land for our mother's kinship with Arthur. Most people think there are three, mind you; or think only three worth mentioning. I recall my aunt, speaking to the king of Dyfed, "Yes, my husband's nephews are a credit to us all. Gawain's a tiger in battle, and Gareth's beautiful – and pious, too – and Agravaine's *so*

9

clever. Oh, yes, and there's Gaheris. He's... dependable."

Spelt gullible. There are worse things. My brothers make enemies, and other people watch out for it. That evening, in the refectory, Gawain glowers and the servants keep clear. It's me he's angry at, for all that. Halfway down his third cup of ale, he sets his knife down, all of a sudden, and stares. "It must stop. D'you hear me?"

Inevitably, I've a mouth full of bread. I say "What?" – it comes out more like "Umphg?"

"Spending so much time on the youngest de Galis. It attracts the wrong kind of attention. And he's a wastrel." He gestures to where Lamorak is barely visible underneath one of the waiting maids.

I look. His hair's a mess, and the girl has her hand inside his shirt. "He's young, Gavin."

"He's got no sense. Now, our Gari..." I catch his eye and look quizzical. "All right, Gari's exceptional. But I..."

"Lady Mahaut."

"I didn't say I was perfect, but..."

"Lady Avise. That girl from..."

"*Stop* it, Heris. All right, he's young. But his family..."

"He can't help who his family is."

"He's taking advantage. You know it." I have never been able to stare Gawain down. "I want you to stop letting him."

"He's not. And anyway, it's harmless."

"His father murdered ours."

Despite myself, I look around before answering. Our father's death has never been a safe subject here. I drop my voice as low as I may, and say, "It was war, Gavin. No one knows for sure. You know that. It could have been Balin. Urien admitted he didn't actually *see* Pellinor..."

"Might have murdered ours, then. Little difference. You're asking for trouble."

I look across at Lamorak, fondling the girl, and sigh. If we carry suspicion and envy from generation to generation, we'll never truly have peace. Ten years ago, the rash youngsters were Gavin and me. One young fool is very like another. Perhaps Lamorak feels my gaze: he looks up, and smiles. I smile back, and, beside me, Gawain thumps the table. A goblet jolts and falls, spilling wine into my lap. Gawain sighs heavily, and hands me his napkin. "Honestly, Heris."

"I'm sorry."

"Hmm." He pauses, chewing on a bite of meat. "Then there's your wife. "

"Oh?" My wife's in love with my brother Gareth. She's never forgiven him for preferring her sister. "I know Luned isn't happy."

"D'you wonder at it, the amount of time you spend with her?"

It's on the tip of my tongue to suggest I take a solo trip to one of my manors, but Gawain's expression suggests that this may not be quite the time for flippancy.

"You leave her too much alone. She feels it."

That's a new one. Perhaps my face shows it, for Gawain looks faintly defensive. "Well, she does. Any woman would. People talk."

Evidently.

"And if you're seen to ignore her... Others may try and make something of it. They think, 'yon lass is lonely', and..."

"And?"

He looks uncomfortable. "Well, they try things."

With sour Luned? This is getting interesting. "What kind of things, Gavin?"

"*You* know." He stares again. My spine starts itching. "Paying court. Making advances. You should stop it."

"I haven't seen it start."

"Exactly. Because you neglect her. You let people get away with too much. Yon Lamorak..."

"Gavin..."

He rides over me, firmly. "Yon Lamorak's been making sheep's eyes at her. She told me so herself."

All the de Galis family are handsome, even quiet Aglovale. Percevale, the middle one, looks like the picture of St George in my mother's book of hours. "Lucky Luned. Perhaps it'll take her mind off Gareth."

"*Ga*heris!" Gawain's voice is too loud. Half the room turns to look at us, and I blush. "This is no joking matter."

No, Gavin."

"The family honour…"

Yes, Gavin.

"You must put your foot down, and stop letting people push you around! "

Overnight, it rains. The ground is caramel-sticky, clinging to boot soles, and miring the horses' feet. The sort of texture that makes the squires uneasy and crimps Kay's long face with a smile. It's warm, too, in that particular way that always makes me feel I should wash more often. I feel thick and disjointed, my hands too swollen to be ready on my sword. Lamorak's wasting his time. Crossing the first court, I skid three times, cursing, and drop my shield.

"Warm, wet and whingeing." The voice belongs to my brother Agravaine. Better and better. "I'm surprised at you. It's perfect weather for ducks." There's less than no point rising to him: it only makes him worse. I just shrug, and keep walking. Gawain's doing, probably. Sent him along to watch me. Guard the family honour.

Maybe *he* can spar with Lamorak. Then at least someone would get something out of this. Me, with luck. Picture Agravaine face down in this mud… Our mother has always said I'm too hard on him… I make myself smile. "Hmm. It's a pity I missed out on the webbed feet." He grins back at me, mocking.

Lamorak is waiting by the postern. The snake eyes are downcast. Well, anyone would have a thick head on the amount he drank last night. When I hail him, he jerks upright. "You're late, Gaheris." And then, frowning, "Oh, hello, Sir Agravaine."

"He's come to see the slaughter. Someone has to take the pieces back."

Agravaine cuts me off. "No, I've come to see fair play. One

can't be too careful with some people."

"You'd know, I suppose," Lamorak says, smiling.

This morning is getting worse by the minute. Getting through the postern, I catch my lanyard on the latch and wind up dropping my shield again. Picking it up, I catch Agravaine in the side with the end of my scabbard.

"You are *such* a fool. Why didn't you bring Evan?"

"He's hungover. Anyway, I hardly need him for this. We're not even armoured."

"You should've been a priest. Good works and lame…"

"Ducks."

Agravaine catches my eye, trying to frown. I hold his gaze a few moments, then mouth *quack*. We both break up, laughing.

Lamorak has got ahead of us, and is already on the practice field, doing fives. He's quick, whipping the blade round, and stopping it with precision. Quicker than me. I may just have reach on him, if I can only keep my footing. I must remember not to hit him too hard, if I can hit him at all, unarmoured as we are. My strength is my only real gift in combat. For the rest… Having Agravaine for an audience is likely to guarantee I wind up flat on my back, even without the mud.

Agravaine is watching Lamorak. After a moment, he turns to me, and his face wears its calculating look. "You're sure you can do this, Heris?"

The buckle on my sword-belt is recalcitrant. "Umm?"

"I could take him for you. There are no witnesses, after all."

"Ouch!" The buckle springs open rather suddenly, and jabs me in the thumb. "What was that, Agrin?"

"I could fight him in your stead."

"I suppose it would be better from his point of view." I look at him, puzzled. "Shall I ask him?"

It's Agravaine's turn to look perplexed.

"Well, he did ask me originally…"

"So what?"

"So, he may prefer…"

"Heris, what does it matter which of us does it? All right, I am the older, but on that argument, it should be Gavin; and as long as father's finally avenged…"

"Avenged?" Sometimes I speak louder than I intend. Lamorak turns to look at us, enquiring, and moves to approach. I wave him back with a hand. "Would you care to explain that?"

Something, some light, drains from Agravaine's face. "My God. Gavin was right, then."

"Right about what?"

"About you and him." Agravaine gestures at Lamorak. "You're just letting him exploit you. And to think I thought… How did I come to be related to someone so stupid?"

"Ask Mother."

"Keep your tongue off her!" For a moment we stand, glaring at each other like over-heated boars. Then he sighs. "You have this golden opportunity… Everyone knows how Lamorak pesters you, and how inexperienced he is. An accident…" I never set out to fight with my brothers. It just happens. My hand is formed into a fist before I realise it. Agravaine watches me, supercilious, superior. "It could still happen, Heris. Maybe you are good enough to kill him. Or bright enough to let me do it for you."

I hit him. I may be heavy, and stupid, and slow, but I'm still bigger than Agravaine. He goes down in a heap at my feet, and lies there gasping. "Get up and say that again."

"And let you knock me down?"

"Why not?"

"Because you're not worth it." He pulls himself backwards on his elbows, and stands up a few feet away. "You'll regret this, Heris."

"Going to tell Mother?"

"I might."

"How brave. The haut Sir Agravaine, hiding behind a woman's skirts."

This time, he charges me. I get his legs in a scissor grip, and we both go down. Over his shoulder, I get a brief glimpse of Lamorak, gawping. Then Agravaine bites me, and I get distracted. It takes a few muddy minutes, but finally I'm kneeling astride him, with his right arm locked behind his back. "Apologise."

His face is half in the mud. Even so, he gasps out "Drop dead."

I'm not feeling obliging. Somewhere off to one side, a voice asks "What's happening", and Lamorak answers "I have no idea." Someone else, disappointed, says "Oh, it's only the Orkneys again."

Lovely, an audience. "Apologise, Agrin."

"No… Heris, you'll break my arm!"

"Good. Maybe you'll learn some manners."

"From you?" He manages to laugh. "I doubt you could do it. *You* can't even bed your wife."

He's my brother… Somehow, I keep my spare hand from his throat.

From behind me, Lamorak says "You filthy liar!", and Agravaine laughs the more. I breathe in, deeply. I must keep Lamorak out of this…

He's standing right behind me. I gesture for him to move back, then rise to a crouch, holding Agravaine at arm's length. "If I let you go, will you get up and walk away?" He lies there, still laughing. "Will you, Agrin?"

"Yes."

"All right… No, Lamorak, stand clear…" I step aside myself, still holding on. Agravaine cheats. "I'm letting go… now."

I'm not quite quick enough. As I let go, Agravaine rolls, and kicks me above the knee. He's laughing as he walks away. "Brother Gaheris. What an idiot."

Lamorak pulls me to my feet again. I'm resigned, but he's white-faced, and trembling. "Why do you let him talk to you like that?"

I'm going to limp for an hour or two. Still Agravaine's black eye will last for days. "He's my brother. Forget it."

"But he treats you like… like…" Lamorak stops, stuck for a word. "And Sir Gawain, last night…"

"Older brothers" privilege."
"You don't act like that with Sir Gareth."
"Gareth doesn't need it."
"And you do?"
"Probably."

For a moment, Lamorak glares, angry less with Agravaine than with me. Then without another word, he turns and walks away.

It's late – midnight or after – when the knock comes at my door.

Evan lies in heavy sleep across the hearth: I too should be sleeping, but I can't. An hour-long lecture from Gawain, followed by reproaches from Gareth and a tearful interlude with Luned have cut up my rest. It's with resignation that I roll off the bed, and answer the door. If I'm *really* lucky, it's Agravaine, back for another round.

Lamorak stands outside, swaying. His clothes are stained, and his face is bruised and blotchy. Blood runs down over one hand, and drips on the floor. He links at me, owl-like. There's enough alcohol on his breath to floor a donkey. He takes a pace forward, then stops. "Did I wake you?"

"No." I don't know what to say, caught here framed in my own doorway. His hair is falling into his eyes: he pushes it back, smearing blood across his face. The effect is grotesque.

"Can I come in?"

He'll wake Evan. "No, Lamorak. It's late."

"But I want to." He looks perplexed. "Please, Gaheris." "No."

His face crumples, child-like. Tears spill over from the snake eyes. He's drunk and he's maudlin. Holy Saints. I could wake Evan myself, and have him fetch Aglovale... "You don't like me. No one does. No one wants me round here."

"Lamorak..."

"You don't want me." His voice is rising: someone is going to be disturbed, and Gaheris of Orkney will take the blame again. "All right, you can come in. But only for a minute or two."

Evan is bound to wake up: I can't let him see Lamorak in this condition… I steer Lamorak into the window embrasure, then go and shake Evan awake. It won't be the first time. There's a girl, from the laundry who visits me sometimes. Evan looks up blearily, and I pull him to his feet. "Go and sleep in the dormitory. I've got a visitor." As I speak, I'm bundling his bedding into his arms. "Go on. Come back in the morning."

Luckily for me, he's more than half-asleep still, and doesn't bother me with questions. I shut the door behind him, and turn back to Lamorak.

"So. What's the matter?" He's sitting on the window sill, looking woebegone. I shall have to do something about that hand. There are bandages somewhere… "What did you do to yourself, anyway? You haven't been fighting?"

"No…" He doesn't sound certain.

"Did you break something? Fall over?" He shakes his head to both. I find clean linen at the bottom of a chest, and start pouring water into a basin. "What, then? You do remember?"

"Yes." He's barely audible. The water's cold, but it'll have to do.

"Want to tell me?" It's too dark in here for cleaning wounds. I light the candles. "Come and sit down over here."

He's trailing blood everywhere. Something else to take care of. He sits down on the edge of my bed, and looks at me, plaintively. The blood is from a deep cut in his right forearm. It's dirty now, but it was made by something clean; a knife, perhaps, rather than a stake, or a potsherd. He winces as I start to wash it. "Well then?"

"Percevale…"

"Percevale did this?"

"No." For a moment, Lamorak sounds almost scornful. Then "He doesn't care enough. He said…"

"Yes?"

"He said it's all my fault."

17

Families. Sometimes I wonder what would happen if they were simply abolished. "What's all your fault?"

"This morning. You fighting with Sir Agravaine."

"He's daft, then. Agravaine and I are always falling out about something. We've been doing it all our lives."

"Yes, but…" He rubs his uninjured hand across his face. "It was because I… Percevale thinks… Lady Luned…"

It takes me a moment or two to work out what he's trying to say. I put a hand on his shoulder, and look into the snake eyes. "It had nothing to do with any compliments you may have paid to Luned. Agravaine and I don't need a reason to argue. We just get under one another's skin. Don't you ever fall out with your brothers?" Was I ever this young? It doesn't seem likely. When I was sixteen we were at war, and Gawain and I were fighting for Arthur against the five kings. Fighting against our own father, Lot, who died in that war at the hand of one of our allies. So Orkney: to fight each other over one thing, then close ranks after the event. Agravaine stayed out of that one, left on Orkney to guard our mother and two youngest brothers. He wasn't there when Lot fell, at Pellinore's hand, or Balin's or God alone knows who. But he remembered, and worked on Gawain, until the latter had no choice but to seek vengeance.

Agrin never forgives or lets go.

No point in telling Lamorak about that. He's too young to remember my father at all, or much about his own, and his older brothers are peaceful men.

I wish Gawain had let Pellinor alone, all the same.

"My brothers and I…. Aglovale's too old, and Percevale's too… Percevale."

Well, when it comes to it, I seldom quarrel with Gareth. "I expect it's the red hair that does it, then. All my family have terrible tempers. Especially when it's raining." That makes him smile. "So. About this cut?"

He looks uncomfortable. "I did it."

"You cut yourself? Why, in God's name?"

"To even things out. I hurt you, this morning." His eyes begin to fill. He's less sober than I'd begun to hope. I've finished cleaning the cut, and am tying off the bandage. "I'm sorry, Gaheris."

"There's nothing to be sorry for." I pour some more water into a cup, and hand it to him. "Now, drink that. It'll help clear your head."

Obediently, he drinks. I start to clean his blood from my floor. He says, softly "My family isn't like yours. We're not... close."

"There's something to be said for that."

"It's lonely." There's silence: in the hearth, a log falls. "What's it like, having brothers like yours?"

"Very noisy, usually."

"I wish I was one of you."

"Do you?" I look across at him. "You might not like it. Our mother... "

He interrupts me. "Gareth. I wish I was Gareth."

"The second-best knight in the world? It's a fair ambition."

"No." Again, he's scornful. "I could be close to you. And no one would mind."

I don't like where this is heading. It happens sometimes that one of the squires or knights" candidate gets to following one of the senior knights. Lancelot, most often, or Bedwyr. Never me. I don't know what to do with this. I say, "Gareth and I aren't so close. I was away to serve Arthur while he was still in the nursery, like you and Aglovale. You should be going back to your room, now, Lamorak."

He ignores me. He's pulled his legs up onto my bed and is sitting with his chin on his knees. "You remember the Chester court? Eight years ago?"

"Not specifically."

"It was midsummer. Mother brought to court for the first time. I was eight years old." His eyes are far away, seeing something outside the room. "It was... I don't know. Another world. There was a tourney. You took the prize."

Now I remember. "Lancelot was away, and Gareth still home

19

in Lothian, and Gawain was so hungover he couldn't ride straight. It was no big achievement. I was just lucky."

"It was everything." Lamorak's voice is fierce. "You're so fair to everyone but yourself!"

"We all get our moment, I suppose."

"Don't…" His voice cracks suddenly, and he hides his face on his knees. Muffled, he says, "You don't understand."

"No." I put the basin back down on its stand, and go to sit beside him. "When I was your age, I worshipped my brother Gawain. He seemed… I don't know, he was so…"

"It's not like that." I'm startled by his vehemence. Startled, and a little afraid. After a moment, he raises his head again, and smiles. It's weak, but a smile, all the same. "I think I drink too much."

"It's possible."

"Will it always be like this?"

"What?"

"I don't know. Life."

"Who knows? You might ask Bishop Dyfrig."

"Yes… Gaheris, may I ask you something? A… boon."

I'm going to regret this. Gawain will lecture and Agravaine will shout. I should say no, but he's giving me the spaniel face again. "I don't know. What is it?"

"At Christmas, I'm to be knighted. Will you stand sponsor for me?"

"That's your brother's place."

"Aglovale won't mind."

"I wouldn't be so sure of that."

"Please, Gaheris."

"It's not that simple. Protocol…"

"I could petition the king."

"No, Lamorak, listen…"

"And you'll train with me? I mean to be the third best knight in the world, after Lancelot and you."

"You mean Gareth."

"Do I?"

Two

It's a fortnight or so later that Kay starts one of his 'improving' conversations after dinner. It's one of those fascinating issues: the ideal of knighthood. What makes a knight, and why. What qualities he should display. Which of the current knights show which qualities, and which, if any, reach the ideal. The queen has retired, but the king my uncle remains at table, listening. I'm not really paying attention: I nurse my ale, and stare into the fire. I'm warm, well-fed, and comfortable. Agravaine has let me alone for the past five days entire. Lamorak hasn't wept on me once. Even the weather's improved: the only cloud is my mother's imminent arrival. We've drawn lots for that, and it's Gawain who's to be the sacrificial host. To Agrin's irritation, and Gareth and my silent relief.

That's not one of the knightly virtues Kay suggests, filial devotion. Saints be thanked. I've enough shortcomings already. His trainees toss the words between them, each anxious to shine, and win the king's approval. There are six of them, due to be knighted at Christmas: quiet Astamore; merry Patrise; Gereint, who's a distant cousin of mine; Amran, oldest of Bedwyr's sons; Osian the poet; and Lamorak. He's unusually quiet, for once, watching his companions.

A handful of the older knights remain, though not all are listening. Bedwyr sits in a corner, smiling as his son, blushing, defends the role of loyalty in a knight's code. Beside him, Lancelot leans on the mantle. Percevale has already held forth for fifteen minutes or more on the need for piety. Lucan the butler cut him off, with a comment on hospitality which made the trainees laugh, and Kay turn his eyes to heaven. The room is blessedly clear of Orkneys, unless one counts my first cousin Ywain, who looks to be asleep.

"But what's more important," asks Osian, "loyalty to one's liege, or to God?"

"It's the same thing," says Amran, shocked. "The king is God's anointed!"

"But if your liege is a duke, say, not the king?" Kay suggests.

"Well, a duke is the king's servant, so…"

"And if he goes into rebellion?"

"You stand by your king!"

"Not your liege-lord? Even though you've sworn a holy oath to uphold him?"

"If he's betrayed his own oath…" Amran looks at his father for help: Bedwyr smiles, and opens his hands. "Well, God can see into all men's hearts, which might…"

"It becomes a matter of conscience," I say quickly. Amran looks relieved. Arthur glances across at me, and smiles. "You have to do what you feel is right."

Kay catches my eye, wickedly. "Whatever the cost? Even at the expense of betraying a kinsman?"

So Gawain chose our uncle over our father. I was his squire back then and I followed him for love and honour. Before I can do more than pull a wry face at Kay, Percevale says firmly "God is the highest liege a man may have."

"That's why a knight absolutely has to…"

"What about courtesy?" puts in Kay, who isn't famed for possessing it. Percevale subsides with a grin, and the discussion veers off on this new tangent.

I top up my ale, and go back to staring at the fire. Perhaps this is why we do it all, for these quiet evenings. Patrise has taken firm hold of the conversation, and is about demonstrating, point by point, that Lancelot is the highest flower attainable by chivalry, and a paragon of all knightly virtues, to boot. Gereint keeps trying to interrupt him with an obscure comment about Tristan, of all people. I'm fervently grateful for the absence of Agravaine. He'd be unlikely to be able to resist the chance to drop hints about loyalty to queens.

"… and Sir Lancelot's honourable, too. His word…"

"Yes, but about Tristan…"

"Shut up, Gereint. Everyone knows that Sir Lancelot's word is as good as a Bible oath. He…"

"This is complete hypocrisy!" The voice is Lamorak's. Lancelot straightens ups, and looks at him speculatively. "You're all sitting here, talking as if he isn't here, praising him to the stars, and he hasn't even blushed!"

"Lamorak…" Kay begins.

Lamorak ignores him. "If he's so good, and noble, and… and so all-round perfect, then…"

"*Lamorak*… "

"No, Kay, let him talk," Lancelot says quietly. I wish Gawain was here, suddenly, or that Ywain would wake up.

"Well, you'd think he'd at least have the grace to look embarrassed!"

Lancelot looks startled. He was, I suspect, expecting something else. Kay chokes on his drink, and has to be thumped on the back by Lucan. There's a silence. Lamorak hesitates, then takes a deep breath. "I'll tell you what makes a true knight."

"Oh, will you?" says Kay, gasping.

"We've been talking round it, all evening." Lamorak sounds defensive. "Courtesy, and altruism, and being merciful, and loyal, and all that… But it's not just having those qualities, is it? It's *how* you have them." Percevale has been frowning; abruptly his face clears, and he looks at his brother with a curious intensity. "The way you make it sound, a knight spends all his time thinking about himself. Doing all those fine things just to show off how noble and knightly he is. Like a competition, or something. Instead of doing them... naturally. Doing them because they're right, and because it serves other people, not to show off, or to beat someone, or to be best all the time."

"Humility, you mean?" says Bedwyr.

"Yes. That's it. And if you start thinking about how things look, or how good you are compared with others, wanting to be top, then you haven't got it, have you? And it doesn't matter if you *are* the best warrior, or the most courteous, or anything, because you're doing it all for the wrong reason. You're doing it for yourself. And, in the same way, it wouldn't matter if you're *not* the best warrior, or whatever, as long as you're doing what you do for the right reasons. Because you believe in the ideal, not in yourself."

There's another silence. Then Percevale says "But God grants skill to His chosen. When a knight acts for Him, then He rewards His servant with excellence, for God's greater glory. And since only God can confer excellence, then..."

"No!" Lamorak glares at his brother. "That's just arrogance. Assuming God favours you just because you happen to be good at thumping people! Assuming someone's better spiritually simply because of feats of arms!"

"Amen to that," Lancelot says, softly.

My uncle the king looks at Lamorak, thoughtfully. "That's a very high ideal of knighthood. But is it possible? Do you think a man can be so selfless?"

"He can try, sire." Lamorak hesitates, then looks at me. Suddenly, I've got a very bad feeling about this.

"And I know someone who does. Without thinking about how it looks, or how good he is, or making comparisons. Just being... who he is."

I'm quite close to the door. Perhaps I can leave without attracting too much attention... Behind me, Kay says "Well, Lamorak, enlighten us. Who is this paragon?"

I *wish* I was faster on my feet. I still don't have my hand on the latch as Lamorak says, scornfully, "Gaheris, of course."

Of course.

"He's kind, and courteous, and always ready to help others – like you, Amran – and he never makes an issue out of his own abilities, but praises other people, and he doesn't try to be top, or to show other people up, and you all make fun of him, and tease him, and he doesn't even mind…"

All eyes have turned to me. My face feels as hot as the fire, and my pulse is pounding. If the floor would only open up. Lamorak pursues his theme relentlessly, "And he's loyal, and honourable, and…"

My mouth is too dry to interrupt. Some-one says *"Gaheris?"* and some-one else answers "Surely not…"

I find my voice, at last. "Lamorak means Gareth. Don't you? It was a slip of the tongue."

"No." Lamorak begins, but I talk over him, blessing Orkney volume. "Gareth, now. I'm his brother, and maybe shouldn't say it, but you'd go a long way to meet his equal – saving your presence, Lancelot. We all know how brave he is, though he'll never admit it, and…" Lamorak is staring at me as though I've just stabbed him, but I don't stop talking until Gereint butts in, and finally makes his point about Tristan.

I stop him, later, as the conversation breaks up. The snake eyes are anxious. "I'm sorry, I'm sorry."

"I've survived worse things. Cheer up."

"I didn't mean to embarrass you. It's just…"

"Forget it."

"But I *didn't* mean Sir Gareth."

"No. But you're still wrong about me, you know. Regardless of… strength of arms, or whatever, I'm no paragon."

"Gaheris…"

"No, listen to me. I have a God-awful temper, and I'm easily as stubborn as Gawain. I'm unfaithful to my marriage vows. I forget fast days, and sometimes I avoid confession for weeks at a time. I have all the Orkney virtues; pride, and vengefulness, and… and damned arrogance about my family. And I do mind when people make fun of me: you saw me fight Agravaine."

Lamorak looks unconvinced. "You always put yourself down."

"I thought you considered that a virtue!"

"I didn't mean..." Lamorak begins, then gives up, and just laughs.

I'm about to follow him from the room, but the king stops me.

"Heris? May I be avuncular and interfering?"

"I've done something stupid again!"

"What? No." He looks faintly rueful. "You shouldn't be so apologetic, you know. Come and sit down over here, and talk to me." I sit. "It's something I've done. I've been meaning to mention it for ages, but somehow..." He shrugs. "You've a knack for blending into the background."

"Handy, in my family."

He considers. "Yes, I suppose so. Agravaine's poor eye!"

"I'm sorry about that. I got carried away."

"Yes, well, I expect he asked for it." I must show faint surprise, for he smiles, and adds "I do know a thing or two about the dynamics of your family."

"Yes, sire. Uncle."

"Anyway... It's about Luned."

Gawain must have been at work. I stare at my feet, and try not to shuffle. "I'm sorry, sire. I do try to make her happy, but..."

"Dear Gaheris. I do wish you'd let me finish."

"I'm sorry."

"She is unhappy, isn't she? Are you?"

"Well, I... It's not as though I had a special lady or anything, before, or..."

"It wasn't fair, was it?" I look up, puzzled. "Poor Luned. I thought it would be for the best, at the time, giving her some status, and you didn't seem to mind, but..." He sighs. "It wasn't, though. I'm very sorry, Heris."

Kings aren't supposed to apologise, even to their nephews. "It's all right, really. I mean, the queen likes her, and..."

He laughs. "Oh, Gaheris! Always trying to make the best of it!" He shakes his head, and looks sober. "The fact is, I should never have forced you into marrying each other. Luned was in love with Gareth, and I rushed her. I should have let her stay here as one of Gwen's maidens for a while, let her settle down, and get over it a bit. Instead... And now she feels hard-done by, and entrenched about Gareth, and she blames you, which is most unfair since it's really *my* fault."

Not Gawain, then. Luned must have been talking to the queen. "I'm sorry. I do try to be nice to her."

"I know you do, but..." He pauses, frowning. "This is going to be the interfering bit, I'm afraid."

"I don't mind."

"No." Again he looks thoughtful. "It's just I've noticed the way you behave with her... If I didn't know better, I'd think she was in the last stages of some terrible illness. Do you think you could treat her a little bit more like an ordinary person?"

"I just worry I'm going to upset her."

"I know you do. But the result is, I don't think she's ever really got to know you."

"I'm sorry."

"Oh, Heris...!" He looks reproachful. "I feel mean, asking. But... Do you think you could court her a little? As if she's just another of the Queen's ladies? Let her see herself as something other than the girl Gareth rejected?"

I hadn't thought of it like that. "Yes, sire. I could try, anyway. She may not like it, though."

He smiles at me. "You've a good heart, Gaheris. Lamorak de Galis was right about that."

"Oh, Lamorak...! He was just talking. He didn't intend anything."

Arthur's expression is quizzical. But, "I wonder?" Is all he says.

"Oh, that's beautiful!"

I'm standing watching the youngsters tilt: Kay's notion of a present to them, a whole day of games. On the field, Lamorak has unhorsed Astamore with a clever double feint. The manoeuvre attracts a ripple of applause. Lamorak looks up and grins. The snake eyes are shining. Meeting mine, briefly, he gives me a high sign, and I shake my head at him. I'm not really expecting a response to my comment, but: "It *was* splendid."

Lancelot, of all people, has come to lean on the railing beside me. His face is thoughtful. My brothers Gawain and Gareth are close friends of this man. They can spend hours together, talking and joking. For myself, I'm foundered in nerves by his reputation. Out in the field, Lamorak and Astamore are squaring up again. I keep my eyes on them. Lancelot says softly, "He has that look to him... that shining quality..."

Like Gareth. Like Lancelot himself. I can't quite keep the pride from my voice, answering. "He is good, isn't he? He wants to be the third-best knight in the world, after you and Gareth."

"Why aim so low?" Lancelot says, and sighs. "He's a credit to you." Surprise makes me look at him.

"To Kay and Aglovale, surely?"

He shakes his head. "Oh, Gaheris... How many hours a week have you worked with him?" I say nothing, picking at a splinter on the rail. "Everyone's noticed. Half the trainees are jealous, and Kay's on at the king to have you made his deputy."

"Lamorak's a natural. I'm just someone to practise on."

"Heaven give me strength! I'm beginning to see why you Orkneys are always fighting each other... Lamorak has aptitude, I grant you, but that's not enough on its own. You've got him to slow down, to think with his head as well as his reflexes."

"I doubt it. Thinking's not my strong suit. Kay..."

"Agrees with me." There's a small silence. On the field, Lamorak has Astamore down again, and is dismounting to fight on foot. Quietly, Lancelot says "I've been thinking about what he said about you."

"Kay?" Waste of time, I'd have thought, unless you happen to be fond of poultry. Still, Lancelot's an odd one. "I took no offence: it was fair comment. My foot-work..."

"I was talking about Lamorak."

Oh.

"The other evening..."

"He didn't mean it. It was just..."

"What he most assuredly did not mean was your brother Gareth."

"Oh, but..."

Lancelot cuts me off firmly. "That boy idolises you. You're his pattern... his *preux chevalier.*"

"I can't think why. He can aim much higher."

"For heaven's sake, Gaheris!" He sounds so exactly like Gawain that I turn to stare at him. So do several other people. For a moment he looks at me in pure exasperation, then he shakes his head. "Now you've got me doing it! Don't you ever have a single, positive thought about yourself?"

"I'm as selfish as the next man."

"Hah!" He pulls a face. "As long as you're standing next to Percevale, or Bors. Lamorak has you almost exactly right. We could all learn a thing or two from your humility."

"That's nonsense." I clench my hands on the rail, and look down. I want to be almost anywhere else.

"What did he say? Courteous, considerate, careful in your dealings with all..."

"I've had more than my share of blood-feuds."

"All of them started by one or other of your incendiary brothers."

"Just stop it!" I don't believe I've just said that, to Lancelot, of all people... "Saints, I'm sorry. I didn't mean..."

"Shut up." I fall silent, but it's a moment or two before I remember to close my mouth. "Lamorak was right. Knighthood isn't just a matter of skill at arms – though you're no fool in that department, either – (no, don't interrupt me). It's a... a question of attitude. A man can be the greatest warrior in the world, and still be nothing, if he forgets his honour, or betrays his duty. And God help him who does that..." His voice trails off. For a moment his face is bleak. He's talking more to himself than me. Then he looks up and says briskly, "The only thing Lamorak missed about you is your damnable naivety. And God knows, if it was a question of Gareth, or Percevale, they'd call it innocence… You're hating this, aren't you?" I say nothing. "I should know better than to lecture you."

"No, I…" I make myself look across at him. "It doesn't sound like me."

"No, I don't suppose it would." Lancelot smiles. "Forgive me?"

"Nothing to forgive." A burst of applause tells me Lamorak has won his round. I hesitate, then "Lancelot, I wonder – could I ask a favour of you?"

"Of course."

"It's not for me, really, it's for him; for Lamorak." Lancelot looks enquiring. "He's got this silly idea about his knighting… He wants to petition the king. Of course, it's Aglovale's place, but for some reason he wants me instead, to sponsor him. And I thought, if you're willing, if you were to offer yourself, then no one would make anything *political* of it, and it would be an honour for Lamorak…"

"He'll refuse."

"Of course he won't. To be sponsored by Lancelot du Lac! I mind our Gareth…"

"Some of them might like the idea, but not your Lamorak." Unexpectedly, he puts a hand on my shoulder. "Gaheris, he wants *you*. Not his brother, or the seneschal, or the soi-disant best knight. It's an honour. You should agree."

"Gawain…"

"Gawain's a reasonable man. Who knows, maybe this is just the thing finally to put an end to that blasted feud. Unless you don't want to?"

I look at Lamorak, garnering congratulations from the other trainees. "My brothers won't like it."

"Confound your bloody brothers!" says Lancelot.

Oh, no.

Oh, no. Three pairs of accusing eyes line up against me, along the wall of my room. All right, two accusing and one baffled, if you make allowances for Gareth. But all the same, my own room is going a bit far. I close the door behind me. "This is nice. Is it my birthday?"

Dear Gareth looks even more perplexed. "I don't think so. Gavin said he wanted a conference, so…"

"My room being smaller than his, darker than yours, and messier than Agrin's, you decided it was the obvious location?"

"Stop trying to confuse Gari." Gawain frowns. "Surely you know why we're here?"

"I daresay I could make a wild guess."

"There's no need to take that tone," Agravaine says. His black eye has healed, more's the pity.

"Oh?"

"I could teach you a better one."

"And earn another black eye?"

Agravaine takes a step forward. Gawain puts out a hand to halt him. "Heris, sit you down. Agrin, stop the insults."

I hesitate. Gareth adds, "Please, Heris?"

Sometimes I think the young and the innocent make the best manipulators.

Gawain waits till I'm seated, then, "We have need of your opinion."

"If," says Agravaine, "you know what one of those is." Gareth kicks him. He frowns, but falls silent.

"Well then, Heris?"

"It might help if you told me *what* you what my opinion on. If it's Agrin, there, for instance…"

"You can stop it, too," Gawain says. I shrug. "It's about Lamorak de Galis."

"Oh, Gavin, not again."

Gawain grins at me. "Lance told me what he said of you. That's a compliment for any man."

"Granted the wit to see it," puts in Agravaine, and Gareth kicks him again.

Gawain ignores the interchange. "Happen, too, I watched the infants' tourney. Lamorak's a fair man with his arms."

"Well?"

"Well, our uncle tells me he's bespoke you as sponsor."

Here we go. "Yes, but I told him…"

"Now, then. It befits a man to hold by his kin, and it's not always a fine thing, choosing another over a brother. But that said, our Gari chose Lance over me, and he's no less our brother for it. Then, too, the king would like it, all of us to be brothers in the fellowship."

"To which Lamorak has not been elected," says Agravaine, "Nor may he live to be."

"Stop your mouth, Agrin, or I'll stop it for you. It comes to this, Heris. I'll not say I'm keen on these sons of Pellinor, but if you want to do it, I'll not stop you. What do you say?"

There's a strong temptation in me to ask him why he needs my opinion on what is, after all, one of his pronouncements. However, Agravaine is making enough trouble for now. So, "You're speaking for yourself, or for the family?"

"The family," Gawain says, over loud sounds of derision from Agravaine. "Leastways, Gari feels as I do, and Agrin *did* say, earlier, that he'd no mind to stop you, umm…"

"From making a public fool of myself?"

"As long as it's quite clear to all parties that I've no part in your folly," says Agravaine, and bows. "But as to Mother, and Medraut…"

"Medraut's not sixteen, yet," says Gawain, as though that settles it.

"And Mother?" Agrin has a point there. Our mother may not have loved our father, but she has a highly-developed sense of property.

Gawain's about to pronounce on this, when there's a knock at my door. Evan, probably. Answering it, I get as far as "What…?" before Lamorak bounces past me, talking a blue streak.

"I was good, wasn't I? I saw you watching, and Sir Lancelot said so, after, though I'd rather have your opinion than his. And he said I could fight on his side at the New Year's tourney, if I liked, but I said I'd rather be on yours, and, oh, Gaheris…"

It's nice to be popular… About this point I manage to break in, by dint of raising my voice rather more than I like to. "Good evening, Lamorak. Will you come in, and greet my brothers."

He stops, then, and looks about him. Gareth smiles. Agravaine is staring at the floor. Gawain just looks at him. "Oh." Lamorak shuffles. "Good even, my lords of Orkney."

"Good even, Lamorak." Gareth is amused. Agravaine simply mutters.

Gawain nods. "Lancelot's no mean judge of fighting men. I might even agree with him. You did well today."

Lamorak looks momentarily nonplussed. Then he remembers his manners, and bows. "Thank you, Prince Gawain." At once he forgets them again. "Oh, but, Gaheris…"

"What did Kay say?" I ask.

That deflates him a little. "That a shield is to be used for parrying, not for waving at people with. But, Gaheris…"

He reminds me of Gareth at this age. Myself, too, I daresay. "You'll do, I expect." Lamorak looks downcast. "You were good."

"Oh, thank you!" For a moment, I'm afraid he's going to hug me. But he controls himself, and merely bounces a little. "And about the big tourney?"

"You're not a knight, yet," says Agravaine, silken-smooth. "What makes you think you can ride with the Orkneys?"

Lamorak looks anxious. Gently, Gareth says "It's a great honour, being asked by Lancelot."

Gawain is watching, thoughtful. "Well, lad? Do you hold yourself good enough to be one of us?"

"But, Gavin, if Lance…"

"Be quiet, Gari. Let the lad speak."

Lamorak draws in a deep breath. Then he looks straight at Gawain. "No, my lord Prince. But the honour of it!"

It's an answer calculated to appeal to Gawain's vanity, and Gawain's smart enough to spot it. Hastily, I say, "Wait, though. Gawain's not fighting. *Will* there be an Orkney side this year?"

Agravaine sighs. "My God. It's true: one must pin something to a lance, and run you through with it before you notice anything." Beside me, I feel Lamorak tense. "Of course there's an Orkney side."

My brother the second-best knight in the world goes faintly pink. "As it happens, our uncle has asked me to be the other leader. But Lance and I thought, for this year, we might pick teams in a less family-oriented way."

"Stupid idea."

"Do be quiet, Agrin, please. For myself, I'd be happy to have Lamorak, if he likes. But I think Lance is meaning to ask Heris."

"Well, lad," says Gawain, looking wicked, "will you go with Gaheris, or do you prefer the honour of riding with Agravaine and Gareth?" Lamorak looks stricken. Suddenly, Gawain laughs. "Let be: I'm teasing. Ride with whoever you please, though happen I was leading this year, I'd choose you, anyway." The light is back in Lamorak's face. "Aye, and my brother will stand sponsor for you, if you wish it still."

He might have asked me… Lamorak makes his very best bow to Gawain, then turns. "Gaheris?"

"What about Aglovale?"

"He doesn't mind. I asked him."

"You could have Lancelot."

"Gaheris!"

I look round at my assembled family. Gareth is still smiling. Agravaine has turned his back. Gawain stares back at me for a long moment, then, all unexpected, winks. "All right, then, Lamorak, but…"

This time, he does hug me.

Three

The next fortnight is a chaos of activity for everyone from the queen down. Rooms that haven't been looked at for eight months are turned out and shaken. Private quarters are commandeered wholesale, and most of us regular residents find ourselves stacked up dozens deep. As two brothers married to two sisters, Gareth and I are packed in together, with one and a half rooms for ourselves, our wives, and brother Agravaine, whose wife Laurel is a cousin of Luned's. We're spared Gawain only by Llinos's pregnancy, which leads the queen to take pity on her, and spare her his snoring. The knights-elect are even worse off: usually they're two to a room, but now all six are squashed into one dormitory along with the junior squires and even some of the pages. Lamorak bewails the impossibility of ever finding any of his particular possessions again. I tell him it's character-forming (one of Agravaine's bouquets), and find it necessary to throw him before he hits me.

The first three times I try courting Luned, she behaves as though I'm in the last stages of insanity. The fourth time, she asks me what I'm up to. The fifth, she hits me, but more in exasperation than in anger; and I make a number of interesting discoveries, not least that there are one or two situations to which brother Gareth's perfect manners just aren't adequate.

Mother arrives, with my appalling youngest brother Medraut in tow, and demands of the king that he start his knightly novitiate immediately. Medraut himself responds by forming an instant passion for Laurel, which distracts Agravaine nicely. Luckily for her other sons, Mother is co-opted to help with the castle-keeping, and more or less leaves us alone. Even with her occupied, though, it's safest to spend as much time as possible as at the far end of the grounds. Some blessed conjunction of circumstances keeps Mother from discovering my exact involvement with this year's knightings, and for once Kay plays right into my hands by anticipating royal consent, and installing me as deputy.

I find I quite enjoy dropping – and being dropped by – trainees into the mud. Llinos wails at the amount of dirt I trail into our overcrowded quarters, and Agravaine congratulates me on having at last found my natural element. In honour of Mother, I refrain from blacking either of his eyes. Lamorak complains, a little, at having to share my attention, but his heart isn't really in it. There's too much going on.

It's my favourite of all the courts, Christmas. The speaking silence of the midnight mass, with all of us lined up in the cathedral, row upon row, united, at peace. And after it, the revelry, with ranks and quarrels put aside, and pages running riot, and Kay uncertain whether to laugh or curse as the conventions fall down around our ears. And the music, and the dancing, and the sudden sweet flirtations… And at New Year the great tourney, with rebated weapons and laughing conflict. It's everything, all folded into a ten-day, and played through at speed. Nothing spoils it, not even Mother. I've not missed a one, since I first came to Caerleon as Gawain's squire.

Until this year. The day before Christmas eve, I misjudge a parry, and catch Lamorak's sword between my shield and my forearm. We're both off-balance: his full weight comes down on me when we fall. I hit my head hard enough to knock myself out, and break my collar-bone and two ribs. He gets away with a few bruises. It's an accident, clear enough, though Agravaine growls, and Aglovale de Galis takes to looking anxious. Lamorak acts as if he's expecting to be tried for murder, and I get to miss most of the festivities. The only consolation is that at least I get a room to myself, on the direction of the court physician. Too much to myself, it turns out, for no one has time to amuse the wounded at this season.

St Stephen's, Kay comes by to see me. The vigil of the new knights will be the next night, with the investiture the day after. It's already been established that I'm to play no part in it. A maimed sponsor is an ill-omen. Kay sits down on my bed, hard, and glares. "You're a bloody trouble-maker, Heris."

"I'm sorry."

"Hmm. Of all the stupid, incompetent…"

"I know, I know. Agravaine already told me."

"Did he? Well, for the first time in his useless life he seems to have a point."

"I'll tell him you said so."

"You do that." He looks at me, considering. "Maybe not. Your Agravaine's got nasty, vengeful habits, and I'm getting too old for all that."

There's not a grey hair in his head. I look at him quizzically for a moment or two, and we both laugh. This hurts. I wind up clutching my side, and gasping. Kay says "Oh, dear," in a tone of the utmost insincerity.

"Just wait… till I can use… my arm again!"

"I'll look forward to it." His face gets serious. "About Lamorak de Galis. "

I haven't seen Lamorak for four days, since Amran and Osian helped me off the field. "What about him? Is he all right?"

"It depends," says Kay, in his worst dark tone, "if you mean all right for normal people, or all right for Lamorak. Whatever *that* is. He spent half of yesterday howling on your brother Gareth."

My family haven't been telling me things. "Oh, Lord."

"Quite. He wants to wait until Easter. He's a screaming failure. He has no honour. He wants to die. You hate him. You'd think he'd just murdered his mother, not fallen on an Orkney! Although now I come to think about it…"

"No blood-feud jokes!"

"Oh, if I must. Though it would make *my* life a whole lot easier if one of you would just tidy him away."

"Kay!"

"All right, all right. I didn't mean it."

"Good. "

"Anyway, I thought I'd come and inspect you, and see if you were even remotely *compos mentis."* Again he looks thoughtful. "Although it's hard enough to tell with you even when you don't have doctors dosing you to the eyeballs."

"Oh, thank you."

"You're welcome. So, are you up to it?"

"To what?"

"Holy Mother! Lamorak."

"It's unlucky… "

"I didn't mean that, you idiot. I meant, are you up to talking to him? He's been trying to get to see you for days, and your brothers won't let him, (and very sensible, too), but now he's started on me…" He shrugs. "I don't want Lancelot complaining to Arthur that I'm being nasty to the poor little trainees again."

"As if you would be!"

"Watch it! Well, can I wheel him in?"

"He's here?"

"Outside the door."

I'm not feeling at my best, if truth be told. The collar-bone isn't too bad, now it's strapped up, but the doctor keeps making me drink foul concoctions that make my head swim, and my ribs ache. I'd love to find an alternative to breathing… Exactly like Kay, to present me with a *fait accompli.* "Is he sober?"

"Yes, of course." I catch his eye, and stare. "Well, he's sober-ish. For heaven's sake, man, it's Christmas!"

"Not so I'd noticed."

"Poor thing! Next time I'll bring you a piece of holly."

"Too kind."

In the brief pause, Kay suddenly grins at me, and produces a half bottle of wine from the floor at his feet. "Just don't tell the doctor where you got it."

He's not such a bad sort, Kay. "I won't. Thanks."

He holds it just out of reach. "And Lamorak?"

I must remember not to laugh. "All right. Let him in."

"I just knew you'd say that. Anyone ever tell you you're a soft touch, Heris?"

"All the time!"

He laughs, and goes to the door. As I find a suitable – and handy – spot for my wine, I can hear him lecturing. "Right. Prince Gaheris will see you. But no dramatics, no vapours, and no tantrums. D'you hear me?" I can't hear Lamorak's answer, but Kay tuts, and says "You'd better mean that, or I'll tell Sir Agravaine where you are."

Prince Gaheris. It's been a while since anyone called me that. Even Agravaine tends to forget his title. Come to it, Lamorak's as much a prince as I am. More, maybe: Nordgwalia's a bigger place than Lothian. Kay ushers Lamorak in, scowling. "Here you are, then. Now, behave yourself."

Lamorak shuffles, and stares at his feet. "Yes, lord seneschal." He might be twelve, not nearly seventeen. Kay snorts, and exits, shutting the door. There's a long silence.

In the end I break it. "Happy Christmas, then, Lamorak."

He looks up at that, and the snake eyes are tearful. Oh, not again... I smile at him, and say briskly, "Surely Kay isn't that bad?" He gives a soft wail, and drops to his knees at the foot of the bed, burying his face in the blanket. Fabulous.

Evan has propped me up with a few pillows, but all the same, it isn't easy to crane my neck to the required angle. "For heaven's sake, Lamorak... Whatever is the matter?"

He gulps, and says something indistinct in which Kay, Aglovale, dishonour and the castle moat are all muddled up together. It makes about as much sense as one of Mother's pronouncements on politics. "Lamorak, do stop it, please, and *talk* to me." No answer. "Will you at least move down this end? You're hurting my shoulder."

At that, he looks up. "Oh, Christ," he says, more distinctly. "I can't do anything right, can I?"

Why must the young be so fragile? I say, firmly, "Don't be daft," and pat the bed with my good hand. "Now, come here and tell me about it. "

He blows his nose on his sleeve, and obeys. "I'm... I'm sorry, Sir Gaheris."

"*Sir* Gaheris? What's this? Respect?"

"No... Yes... I messed up again, didn't I?"

"I don't know. What have you done?"

"What have I done?" He looks at me, appalled. "What haven't I?"

"Killed someone? Insulted a lady? Perjured yourself?"

"No, but..."

"Well, then. Dear Lord, Lamorak, you have got to learn to stop over-reacting to the least thing, or you'll draw yourself more trouble than you can handle." The snake eyes are doubtful, looking at me. "All this, because a middle-aged knight made an idiot's parry?"

"You're not middle-aged."

I'm twenty eight. "Well, maybe not. But I *am* an idiot." He opens his mouth to contradict. "Any junior squire knows not to parry like that. I was stupid, and now I'm paying for it. But you haven't 'messed up', or crippled me, or dishonoured yourself. It was an accident."

"But..."

"Not everything you do will be glorious, or tragic. Sometimes things just happen." No need to tell him now how much accidents may cost. He'll find out. "You don't need to dramatize everything."

"That's what Sir Kay said."

"Well, he's right."

"Yes..." He hesitates. "They wouldn't let me see you, and Sir Agravaine said... If you died, he..."

I'm going to give Agravaine considerably more than a black eye. I have to keep the anger from my voice, answering. "Well, I'm not intending to die. This time."

"No." Abruptly, the snake eyes overflow again. "Oh, Gaheris." He lifts my good hand and hugs it to him. "Kay said you weren't... and Sir Gareth... but..."

"I've done myself more harm falling off my horse. Oh, Lamorak, do stop it."

He sniffs, hard. "I'm sorry."

"That's better. I'm sorry, too. But it's done, and must be lived with." I manage to get my hand back, by dint of some wriggling. "I'm afraid I've let you down."

He straightens up somewhat, and seems to be making an effort. "I wanted to wait for Easter, but no one agreed."

"Quite right, too."

"Do you really think so?"

"Of course."

"But..."

"Why delay something so major for the sake of a two-hour lecture while you're sitting in your bath?"

That makes him laugh. Then he says "But a sponsor... It's more than that, surely?"

"No. How do you think all the people who get knighted in the field manage?"

"I hadn't thought about it."

"Well, then." I gaze at the foot of the bed, thinking. "It's... it's a formality, really. Like checking you've got your shield before riding out. To remind you what you're taking on." Remember Gawain, looking momentous... "Aglovale's a fine man; he'll make a grand sponsor."

"I'd rather have you." Lamorak sounds wistful. "What were you going to say to me?"

"I'm not sure... Try to be fair, to yourself and others. Keep your word, to king and country. Remember to parry with your shield, not your elbow." He smiles. "That sort of thing. What

Gawain said to me, more or less (except the bit about parrying)."
Strange how some things stay with you. I can still remember the
narrow room, the feel of cooling water, Gawain's face in the
firelight...

"What did he say?" Lamorak asks. He's watching me with an
odd intensity, as if he's waiting for something.

"That's a long time ago." All that time as Gavin's squire. We
were closer, then. Before all this blood-letting began. Perhaps I'm
silent a long time, for Lamorak begins to look worried.

"Are you in pain?"

"I'll do." He still looks concerned. "I was trying to remember,
that's all." He relaxes a little. "Well, then..." When I try, I still have
the accent of my childhood, that we all have in stress, and Gawain
more than most. "Something like this: 'Love your king – and God
– and your own kin. Stick by what you know to be right, and don't
go chasing follies. Keep your sword clean, and your honour with
it, and never forget whose arms you bear. Be polite to women – all
women, not just ladies, mind – and watch your tongue with your
elders and betters. Happen you'll disagree, betimes, but see you
keep quiet – and that means you must mind Agrin, as well as me,
and don't go pointing out mistakes we can see by ourselves. Don't
take an insult; but don't go looking for them, neither. And never
refuse an adventure, or a fair request – although mind you don't
go making yourself a martyr to all comers, for you will go letting
others put on you. And see you wash regularly, and don't go doing
all the damn fool things I did!" By the end of this, Lamorak's
laughing helplessly.

"Did he really say that – about washing?"

"Aye, man, happen he did."

He laughs some more. "And you were going to say that to me?"

"Well, maybe not the bits about washing, and listening to Agrin
– to Agravaine. And there might have been a thing or two I'd add
for you yourself, as Gavin did, when he told me to stand up for
myself." I sigh. "There's a lesson in that, if you like, for he's still
saying I don't and telling me I should."

Again that intensity in Lamorak's face. "Do you think he's right?"

"Who knows?" Shrugging is nearly as bad as laughing. "It's just his way of telling me to do right – and to have right done by me."

"I hadn't thought of it that way." Lamorak looks thoughtful. "What would you say just for me, then?"

"Aglovale… "

"I want to know!"

There's such urgency in his voice that I jump. "Why does it matter so much?" He gazes at me for a long moment, then looks away, shaking his head.

"I can't explain. I just… I can't tell you." I can hear his breathing, quick and ragged. There's something here I don't understand.

"You feel things too much. You need more… I don't know, more sense of *proportion*. You care too much."

"Do I?" He laughs mirthlessly.

"Well, maybe you don't. I don't know. All I know is that you're very different to me."

"Am I?"

"I think so. I'm not very good at understanding people." Lamorak is silent. Suddenly there's a tension between us, and I can't see why.

With sudden ferocity, he says "I don't want you to understand!" And then, "No, I do want it!" He draws in a long breath, and turns round. "Tell me: what do you think of me?"

I can't help smiling. "That you have an incorrigible habit of fishing for compliments." He bites his lip. "Dear heaven, Lamorak! You're a very promising young knight."

I expect him to seize on the compliment, in his usual fashion. Instead, he looks down and shuts his eyes. His face is bleak. I'm afraid for him, suddenly. There's a shadow across the light that Lancelot spoke of, a darkness. "Lamorak?" He makes no answer. I'm not equipped to deal with this… I need Gareth… He's right, I don't understand.

It's Gawain who breaks the spell, opening the door and entering. I jump. "Rescue squad," he says, cheerfully. "Kay said you'd need it." Lamorak beside me swallows hard, and rubs a hand across his eyes. Gawain looks at us. He's slightly drunk, which emphasises the accent. "Christ, man. Will you look at the pair of you! There's someone dead, is it? You willna learn, Heris. You will go letting yourself be put on."

Beside me, Lamorak gives a laugh that turns quite suddenly into a sob.

I persuade the doctors to let me out of bed for the tourney. They don't argue too hard: maybe even they are softened by the Christmas spirit. My brothers are delighted. Now Gawain can fight, and I (oh, joy!) can field Mother. She's on form. As I settle myself under the royal canopy, she's already in full flow, talking and eyeing up the young men. Agravaine holds she's beautiful. I'll grant she has a fine way of grabbing attention. I'm a poor substitute for Gawain; she's already made that plain. One can, I suppose, be thankful for these small mercies.

Her daughters-in-law cluster round her. I'm not really listening, but the giggles suggest that the conversation is typically scandalous. To my left, my aunt catches my eye, and smiles sympathetically. "Poor Gaheris. Are you feeling very left out?"

"Not really." I smile back. "Look at the company I'm getting to keep. "

She pulls a face. "Quite. I'm relying on you, though. You'll have to help me judge, since Arthur has abandoned me." My uncle has, for once, exercised privilege, and taken the field with Gareth's side.

"I'd be honoured."

"Bless you, Heris; you're a treasure." She looks at Mother, briefly. "And a welcome relief from gossip." Her expression is just a little wicked. "So. Who do you think will win?"

I have to think about that. It's pretty even this year, though

Lancelot may have gained some advantage in replacing me with Gawain. "I don't really know."

"Diplomat! Who'll take single honours, then, since both Gareth and Lance have exempted themselves."

"Gawain, of course." She laughs. "Well, maybe Palomides."

"Agravaine," puts in Mother determinedly, "is not to be discounted lightly. He looks very good to me." He would. He's wearing her favour. "You always underrate him, Gaheris." I shuffle my feet and do my best to avoid her gaze. She goes on, "Some of my sons are a credit to me, anyway."

"Yes, Mother." She glares. I've forgotten again, not to call her Mother in public. It reflects badly on her age. "I'm sorry."

"Well, that's normal."

"Agravaine is certainly looking handsome," my aunt says, hastily. "I'm not surprised you're proud of him. And you, too, Laurel."

Mother preens. Laurel, overshadowed, says nothing. Llinos says loyally, "Well, I think Gareth looks marvellous", and everyone smiles.

"I have such attractive children," Mother says, complacent. "Do at least try and keep out of my light, Gaheris."

Gawain has ridden his horse two circuits of the field: now, he reins in before us, and bows. Lamorak follows him, hovering. He looks nervous. Under cover of Gawain's salutations, I catch his eye, and smile.

He's white. "Good day."

"And to you. Don't look so worried. It's only a friendly competition. It's been years since anyone died."

He gives me a dusty look. "I think I'm going to be sick."

"You shouldn't drink so much."

He looks startled. "No... Gaheris?"

"Lamorak?"

"I was wondering... Since it's my fault... That you're not out here, so I..."

"I thought we'd agreed not to apportion blame."

"No, please... Would you let me carry the Rose-Knot for you?"

The Rose-Knot is my device: Lamorak as yet has only his blank shield. Gawain has already asked me the same question, and received the same reply. "I don't think so."

"Oh, but..."

"It isn't necessary. Or appropriate."

"But I wanted..." He looks at me, snake eyes pleading.

I have to be gentle. "It's a kind thought. But I'll have other days, and this is your very first tourney. You should act in your own name."

"Are you sure?"

"Yes."

"Oh." He hesitates. Gawain has already made his farewells, and is riding back to be mustered in by Lancelot. Lamorak says "Then..."

"Yes?"

"With your permission... If I might address Lady Luned..." She turns, hearing her name, and Mother looks round with her. "My lady, I'm at least partly responsible for depriving you of seeing your lord win glory for you today. As some slight recompense, would you honour me with your token instead, so that I may try to redress the wrong?"

It's a pretty speech: the smile that accompanies it is devastating.

Luned, turning to me, misses it, giving Mother the full benefit. Lamorak waits a moment, then adds, "Please?"

"Why, how charming," Mother says. "And so proper. Be kind to him, Luned. I would."

Luned still hesitates. Lamorak says, "It would be in Prince Gaheris' name, of course. I mean no impropriety."

"Charming," repeats Mother.

He looks so vulnerable... It's a very smooth act. Luned is wavering: her hand twists in her veil. I look at sly Lamorak, and shake my head. Then I smile at my wife, and say, "I wouldn't mind, if it's your wish."

"Oh, you must," Mother says, and smiles at Lamorak. "I'd give you my token, were Agravaine not already wearing it."

He bows. "I'm honoured, your majesty."

He's a twicer… Luned has unfastened the veil. Leaning forward, she offers it to him. "Here, then."

Taking it from her, he makes an issue out of kissing her hand. "Thank you, gracious lady." Another bow, then a look at me. "Gaheris…"

"They're nearly mustered. Go on, now."

"Yes…"

"That's a very pretty child," Mother says, as he rides away. "And so gallant. Not like you: you were a late starter." I keep quiet. "Whoever is he?"

"Lamorak de Galis. Pellinor's youngest."

"Is he, now," says Mother, and her eyes linger on Lamorak.

He doesn't disgrace Luned's token. Gawain, too, upholds a private promise, and gives Agravaine a hard fall. Palomides carries the palm. The new knights all give good accounts of themselves, and all escape injury, so no one must be left behind when they leave, two days later, for their year's errantry.

They always go at dawn. In the cold and damp, it's usually only close kin who rise to see them off. Even so, despite my shoulder, I prevail on Evan to wake me, and make it down. Bedwyr grins at me, and Ywain raises a brow.

He's there for Gereint. I greet them, and spend a few minutes discussing his intended route. Beside me, Mador de La Porte is lecturing Patrise and Astamore. Lamorak is all but invisible between his brothers.

"You're early," says a voice in my ear. Kay. "Learning the ropes? Very diligent."

"Something like that."

"Hmm." He's looking at Lamorak. "Worthy. Most worthy."

"My best quality."

"Really?" He pulls a face, and we both laugh.

"Ouch. Well, maybe my second-best." Aglovale has turned to speak to Osian: over his shoulder, I see Lamorak looking round. The snake eyes are anxious. Then he meets my gaze, and, quite suddenly, his face clears. No smile, but some other thing... Think of Llinos, seeing Gareth safe home...

No.

Percevale, too, has noticed me. Being Percevale, he bows, and offer me an arm. Once accepted, he conducts me to Lamorak, and leaves us alone. There's a small silence.

"They should patent him... Are you ready to go?"

"Not really." Lamorak grimaces. "Travelling in mid-winter."

"New Year's the right time for making beginnings."

"Is it?" He looks pensive. "Is it right to begin with a parting?" I've no immediate answer to that. It's not an angle I'd ever considered. "Well, it's not really a parting. You'll be coming back soon enough." Most of them, anyway. Almost every year, there's one or two...

Don't think of that.

He smiles, twisted. "So I will." I've heard Agravaine sound more sincere. "There's something to look forward to."

He should be excited. Not this tension. Behind us, I hear Patrise's quick Irish voice bubble and laugh. Amran is grinning as he listens to Bedwyr. Suddenly Lamorak takes hold of my good arm and stares straight at me. "Oh, Gaheris, I can't."

"Don't be daft."

"But if I go... I won't..."

"I thought you were going to be the third-best knight in the world."

"Oh, that! What's that, compared to being without..." He trails off, but I've a glimmer of a notion as to his problem.

"If she loves you, she'll wait."

"What?"

"Whoever it is you can't do without." He looks unconvinced.

"She'll still be here when you get back. If that's what's bothering you."

"Sort of." I can't make sense of his expression. "And if... she... doesn't wait?"

"Then she doesn't deserve you."

"Oh, God, you would say that!" His laugh is a little hysterical. "Though I expect you're right."

"I'm quoting Gawain, so I must be."

"I've never thanked you, have I? For all your time and help."

"It's nothing." I don't like to be thanked. Pink doesn't mix with sandy hair and freckles. "Forget it."

"Never." His intensity unnerves me. "I'd count that dishonour."

"It really isn't that important. So, do you have everything you need to take with you?"

"Yes, almost." He releases my arm. I step back. "Plus a lot of advice from Percevale that I really don't need."

"I can imagine. I recall Agravaine giving our Gareth a half-hour lecture on pavilion etiquette alone."

"He didn't mention that one." Lamorak looks wicked. "Shall I ask him?"

"Percevale? Saints, no!" I think. "Aglovale, though..."

"Indeed?" The snake eyes narrow. Twisting round, he taps his brother on the shoulder. "Loval, what's all this I hear about your lady- killing exploits?"

"What?" Aglovale looks stunned.

"I have *very* good authority. My lord prince Gaheris tells me..." My lord prince Gaheris is doing his damnedest to look innocent.

Aglovale makes his excuses to Osian, and joins us. *"My* lady-killing exploits? That's a good one, Liam, after what you've got up to round here. And as for you, Gaheris..."

"I was just making polite conversation."

"Oh, well, that explains it." Aglovale de Galis is an odd one. Even Agravaine has never been able to pick a fight with him. Now he favours me with an amused glance. "Gaheris is an expert."

"No, I'm not. I'm married."

"A *married* expert…"

"All right, all right. I'm sorry. I was only trying to explain to Lamorak about pavilions."

"The first rule is *never* to get into a bed in one unless you're quite sure it's empty first."

"Or looking for trouble."

"Or for Lancelot." Our *parfait gentil knight* has made a fool of himself that way a time or two: Aglovale and I catch each other's eyes, and laugh. Lamorak looks cross. Aglovale pats his shoulder. "All right, little brother. The grown-up knights will stop behaving like children." Lamorak doesn't look convinced. "I'm sorry, Liam." Behind him, several of the others are already mounted. Patrise is adjusting a stirrup. "All set?" Aglovale asks.

"I think so." Lamorak sounds nervous. "At least…" Abruptly, he stops, and hugs his brother.

Aglovale aims a mock punch at him. "Off with you, then. I want my breakfast. Give 'em hell, all those recreant knights… Have you said goodbye to Piers?"

I step back some more, and try to wave to Gereint. He doesn't see me.

It's only as he's about to leave that I realise I've said no farewells to Lamorak. He looks the part; the compleat knight-errant. He'll be fine. The cold is hurting my shoulder. I watch a moment or two more, then turn to go. There's a great turmoil of hoof-beats and goodbyes: I'm on the stair before I notice my name being called.

Lamorak has ridden his horse to the foot of the flight: we're almost on eye-level. "Gaheris?"

"Yes?"

"You didn't say goodbye."

"Goodbye, then."

"Yes." He bites his lip. "I will see you? Next year?"

"God willing. Maybe even in the summer, if our paths cross."

"I hadn't thought of that." His face lights up. "The summer, then."

"Perhaps."

"I can hope." He hesitates. "Gaheris?"

"Yes?"

"I wanted... He reaches a hand out. I come down a step or two to clasp it. "Will I make it?"

"Who knows? I think so." The others have all left. "If you ever set out in the first place, that is."

"Well, I have to." Again, that pause. "Could I... would you...?"

"What?"

"It's just that..." Quite suddenly, he leans down from his horse, and tugs one of my gloves out from where it's tucked through my belt. The other falls to the ground. "Can I have this?"

I'm not comfortable. It makes me irritable. "What for?"

"Please, Gaheris."

"I'm not sure I..."

"It's to remind me."

"What about?"

"Of... of the right way to parry. Shield, not elbow."

This is ridiculous. He has on his spaniel look. "Oh, all right. But it's silly." He smiles. I add, "God speed you."

"Thank you. You're not cross?"

"Only a little."

"I'm sorry, then. I'll see you. In the summer." He turns his horse's head towards the gate.

"That's not certain," I call after him, but he doesn't seem to hear.

Kay has to pick up my other glove for me, from where it lies on the ground.

Four

It's not a long winter, nor a cold one. My bones heal clean, and I'm kept busy by my new duties. Brother Medraut proves to be the worst aspect of these. He's the most apt of the new squires, but his tongue would cut stone. I'm torn between fraternal pride, and a pure desire to wring his neck. Llinos's child is a girl, and Gareth insists on calling her 'Lancella', for his hero. The rest of us laugh at him, except Agravaine, who wanted her named for Mother. The latter stays with us until Easter, which is a delight for some, and a burden for many. I'm not the only one breathing the easier for her departure in early spring.

Intermittently, there's word of our new knights. Someone bumps into one of them, or they send tidings back. All alive, all doing well. The first of the overthrown foes to come and pledge himself to Arthur is sent by Gereint, to Gawain's delight, but one comes from Lamorak not long after. From then on, he seems to send one almost every other week. They all bring the same message: "Sir Lamorak de Galis has vanquished me, and sent me hence to swear eternal allegiance to his lord King Arthur. Oh, and I've a message from him for Prince Gaheris of Orkney."

After the third or fourth, Kay gets to calling them "Lamorak's love letters", and I'm obliged to give him a fall on the wettest part of the tourney-field.

I'm too busy to ride out that summer, and it's Christmas before

I see Lamorak again. He rides in on Christmas Eve, with Palomides' brother Safere, and Astamore. They're the last, save for Amran, and they're made much of. It's hard to tell which of the girls clustered around Lamorak is the special one.

He's grown a beard, and has the remains of a bruise along one cheek bone. He's taller, too, standing nearly on eye-level with me. Not that I see so much of him: there are a lot of people bidding for his time, and I have my hands full with the trainees. He is most often with Safere, and sometimes Tristan, who's honouring us with his company this year. Every so often, I feel myself watched, and look up, to find eyes on me. Occasionally, it's Lamorak; more frequently it's Safere, which perturbs me a little. I don't know why.

Agravaine finds this funny, for some reason.

Mother chooses to spend the festival with Aunt Morgan, which only adds to the pleasures of the season. Medraut takes himself off to visit her, with cousin Ywain. Kay and I open a book on how many quarrels they're likely to have. The rest of us Orkneys combine with a number of the other Northerners for the New Year tourney, and astonish everyone except Gawain by taking the day. He wins the solo prize, too, after disarming Lancelot and wrong-footing Bedwyr. Even Agravaine is laughing as the hall is decked with Orkney pennants: Gavin's Pentangle, Agrin's Sunburst, Gari's Lion-and-Lamb, and my own Rose-Knot. He has Bors to his credit, and a set of bruises to remind him. My own bruises bear testimony to a show of determined aggression by Sagremore and Safere. The latter refuses to shake hands, after, and stays away from the feast. Agravaine finds that funny, too.

It's two mornings later that I find Lamorak lying in wait for me in the south vestibule. He puts a hand on my arm, and stops me. "Come riding with me, Gaheris?"

The snake eyes are bright and guileless. "Good morning, Lamorak."

"Yes, yes. Will you?"

"I have things to do. Duties. Later, maybe."

He takes his hand away, abruptly dignified. "Forget it. I am sorry to have troubled you, Prince Gaheris."

It's far too early in the day for moods. "Have it your way, then."

"Oh, I wish!"

"What?"

"All I wanted was a chance to ask you in private just why you've been avoiding me. But if you're too ungenerous to grant even that...!"

"I beg your pardon?"

"You know what I mean!"

"No, I don't." We're beginning to attract attention. "Do calm down, Lamorak." I hold a hand out to him: he ignores it.

"You're deliberately trying to humiliate me!"

The Orkney temper is not always an asset. I have to struggle to keep my voice level, answering. "No. I assure you I am not doing that."

"You're a liar."

If Agravaine said it, I'd hit him. Lamorak isn't my brother. Ten or twelve witnesses have heard the insult... As lightly as I may, I say it. "No, I don't think so," and I start to walk away. I'm shaking. Now would not be the best time for a display of Orkney temper. All the same, I don't understand, entirely, what is happening.

"Don't walk away from me," Lamorak calls after me. I keep going. I don't trust myself to answer him. Behind me, voices are starting to murmur, and Lamorak shouts my name again. Gareth would have handled it right. Gareth would never find himself in the middle of a public quarrel... Half the court has heard me called a liar, and seen me take it... I slam a fist a few times into a convenient hay-bale, and swear. Gaheris the incompetent does it again. If Agravaine needed an excuse to warm up that old feud, he has it now.

Wonderful.

My hand hurts.

It takes me a few minutes to get myself back in control. Then I grit my teeth, and go back inside in search of Lamorak. I find him the refectory, glaring into a goblet. Safere is with him. So are a number of other people, including (lovely) Tristan. All I need is *his* indiscretion… Safere looks up, and his eyes narrow.

I'm unarmed. Perhaps it's for the best. When I stop in front of the table, Safere makes a gesture to wave me away, but I ignore him. "My lord Prince Lamorak."

He doesn't answer. Tristan gives me one of his rueful grins, and says, "Rotten timing, Gaheris."

"Quite probably." Tristan raises an eyebrow. I raise my voice, and repeat myself. "Prince Lamorak."

Of all my family, I have the least public grace. When I still receive no response, it's in me to give up and walk away. Then Safere smiles at me. Mother should practice that much malice.

Here goes nothing. "Prince Lamorak. I have offended against you. I was wrong. Therefore, I render you my unconditional apology; and I pray you will do me the honour of accepting it." My voice should have carried to the furthest point of the room. Agrin's going to love this. Safere's smile vanishes, and he regards me thoughtfully.

Lamorak still doesn't answer. I bow, then, and prepare to go.

Safere's light voice stops me. "Admirably tactful, but quite unnecessary, in the circumstances. Very surprising." He leans back on his bench, and draws a finger along his jaw. "Little snake is sulking. Little snake knows he doesn't deserve apologies when he's childish." His eyes flick up and down me. "So perfectly charming."

He manages what I could not: Lamorak looks up. He's scowling. "Shut up. Saf. This is none of your business."

"Indeed not? Shall relief overwhelm me?" There is in Safere's voice all the compassion of wire rope. He turns back to me. "I shall not pretend I like you, king's son of Orkney; but I grant you this much. You are doubly fair. There are those who are not."

Well, I don't like Safere, insofar as I know him at all, either. And I've never been any good at riddles. I mutter something non-committal, and begin to back off. Lamorak goes on glaring at Safere for a few moments, then rises, and follows me. "Gaher… My lord prince… "

"Yes?"

"He's right. Safere. I'm at fault. I..." He hesitates, looking round him, then raises his voice. "Please accept my apology."

I'm wary. He's too much trouble, this morning... But half the hall is still watching us, so I bow, and offer a hand. "Of course. What is all this, Lamorak?"

He looks over his shoulder. "It's just that... Are you really avoiding me?"

"Don't start that again."

"No, I'm sorry. It's..." Again the pause. "Can you really not spare me a few minutes?"

Here we go again. Well, I suppose Kay can do without me for one morning. "All right. But no dramatics."

"No... Can we go out of here?"

I shrug, and we make our way out in self-conscious silence to the stable. It's only as we're riding along the track from the postern that Lamorak sighs, and says "It's the one reliable thing, isn't it? I make trouble for you. And I never intend to."

"I don't suppose I think you do."

"Is that why you put up with it?"

"No." He looks concerned. I say, "It's simply that I don't like scenes. I'm lazy."

"I see." He sounds disappointed. "Is that why you've been avoiding me?"

"I thought we agreed... Oh, all right. I hadn't noticed that I *was* avoiding you. What makes you think I am?"

"I came back, and... You didn't seem pleased to see me, and you were always busy, and..."

"Well, I am busy these days." It isn't a satisfactory answer. "I don't know, Lamorak. It wasn't deliberate. But you have your own place, now. And I suppose I saw you with Tristan, and so forth, and we've never got along... It's lots of little things. People grow up, Lamorak."

"Even me?" He smiles. "Is that a hint?" I don't say anything. He goes on, "Well, it's fair comment, I suppose. When I was away... It never occurred to me that things would be changing here, too. And when you didn't show up in the summer, I thought… "

He stops, and shakes his head.

I look across at him curiously. "That was never a promise. As it turned out, I didn't have time to leave court. I didn't even get out to any of my own holdings. I assumed you'd realise that."

"You hadn't forgotten, then?"

"No."

"Safere thought you had. And Margawse – I mean, your lady mother – said that Sir Agravaine… That is…" He has twisted his reins around his fingers; he won't look at me. "She thought it possible that Sir Agravaine had told you certain… details that weren't to my credit. "

Mother is a trouble-maker. Pellinor must once have turned her down. "Agravaine says a lot of things about a lot of people. Usually I ignore him."

"But did he say anything about me and… Well, anything…?"

I frown; I can't remember anything that struck me as being above Agrin's usual level of malice. Nearly everyone young and promising is an effeminate fool in my dear brother's eyes. "Nothing I specifically remember, no."

"I see." He looks at his fingers trapped in his reins, and laughs. "I'm idiotic, then."

"You said it." Something occurs to me. "You saw my mother?"

"Yes, I…" He stops, and to my astonishment, I realise he's blushing. "I was a guest of hers at Belmotte for a while. She was very kind to me."

Oh, was she? Well, that explains the apparent disappearance of his special lady here. Trust Mother. He's far too young for her. And if one of my brothers gets to hear about it… "I wouldn't build too much on her kindness, if I was you. She's, umm, kind to a lot of people."

He shuffles. "I enjoyed her company."

I shouldn't listen to this. "Hmm. Just don't tell any of my brothers."

"No." He looks up at that. "I do know that much."

"I should hope so."

He's looking thoughtful. "I did like being with her, you know. She made me feel... less isolated."

I'll bet. I favour him with my best sardonic look. "Well, it's your funeral."

"I hope not!"

"Be careful, then." Blast the woman. Let's just hope that winter court will take his mind off her. We ride on in silence in a few moments, then I raise an issue that's been on *my* mind. "Lamorak, do you happen to know why Safere doesn't like me? I barely know him."

"I didn't know he didn't."

I don't quite believe that. "He said so not an hour ago."

"Oh, that." Lamorak looks awkward. "Well, you overthrew him at the tourney... "

"If I held a grudge against everyone who ever defeated me, I'd have no one to talk to!"

"I don't know why, then. Why do you expect me to?"

"No special reason. I thought he was a friend of yours."

"He's all right." He sounds defensive. He won't look at me.

"I didn't say he wasn't. What's the matter?"

"Nothing." He pauses, then takes a deep breath. "I think I just... I've been on my own so much, and now it seems so crowded here." I understand that one: I smile at him reassuringly. He continues, "And the whole time I was away, I missed being here so much. And now it's all different."

"Not completely."

He smiles. "No. Not completely."

Amran doesn't come back.

Ever after, the time that follows is known in family memory as 'Gaheris' good year'. Perhaps it's all the practice. Perhaps it's just a change in my luck. Whichever, for a while the old awkwardness falls from me, and I find I have an aptitude I formerly lacked. It's interesting, though I'm not wholly sure I like it. The winter is quiet enough, apart from Mother's visit. Lamorak hangs around her rather more than is strictly wise, and I have to caution him before Agravaine notices and takes umbrage. He's already cross enough with Lamorak: the latter has trounced him twice in tourneys, and picked three fights with Medraut. The cause of this turns out to be insults to me. I can't take Lamorak in the field, but I still weigh more than he does: it takes me three-quarters of an hour and a lot of bruises, but eventually I have him convinced to leave my family quarrels alone. In the summer, Kay and I get grace to ride errant, and wind up tangling with a fair cross section of the Cornish knights. Somewhat to my discomfort, the local sub-king, Marcus, takes it into his head to pull Lancelot's stunt of riding incognito, and I give him a hard fall. Luckily, he thinks it funny. I rather wish Lancelot had never started that fashion. It can get embarrassing.

Three weeks later, I resort to it myself. We've seen several of our companions, but heard nothing of Lamorak. He left somewhat later than we did, waiting for his brothers, and intending to ride west. But in mid-August, Kay and I come on two pavilions pitched in a largish clearing next to a ford. It's a good spot for casual sport: indeed as we round the hill-crest, we can see two knights practising in full kit. One of the shields – a snake curled about a stylised rose – is unfamiliar to me. The other is Safere's. Oh, joy. I've fought him three times since Christmas, and won every time, but his hostility unnerves me. Worse, he was travelling with Tristan, the last I heard. Tristan doesn't like the Orkneys. It's not his shield, granted; but he's one who makes a habit of disguise.

Well, there's no way out of it. And Kay beside me is cheerfully preparing himself for a friendly bout. If anything involving Safere can be said to be friendly...

I look across at him hopefully. "Umm..."

"Let me guess. You want to swap shields?"

"If you don't mind. It's just that Safere... But I think the other one's Tristan... Of course, if you feel more glory..."

Kay shields his eyes with his hand. "No. He's too slim to be Tristan. I think it's Andred. You know, that bloody cousin of Marcus'? He has a different device every time I see him. So, *do* you want to swap?"

He's looking at me quizzically. I shuffle a bit, and say "Yes."

"The things I do for you!"

"I know. I do appreciate you."

"Oh, really?" He raises a brow. Then he passes me his black tower shield.

I hand him the Rose-Knot. "Thanks, Kay. You're a good friend."

"Tell that to my contusions. Safere has a spite against you, Sir Duck."

"Quack." Kay pulls a face. "I had noticed."

"You and the rest of the court." He pauses to pull down his visor. "Shall we?"

"Lead on, foster uncle!"

Our direction of approach gives us a slight advantage: because of the rise, the knights encamped below don't see us until we're almost upon them. There's a brief instant of chaos, then Evan yells "Give passage to my lords!", and Safere's Aidan yells back "Not without they fight mine, if they have the courage for it!"

I'm still trying to place the serpent-rose from the style of his riding, when his lance point impacts neatly with my shield, and punts me off my horse.

Well, I've been expecting to come back to the ground sooner or later... I pick myself up, duck out of Kay's path, and draw my sword, as the serpent-rose comes back round for another go. He's fast, but he's not a master horseman... he has a slight problem managing reins, shield and lance. I wait till I think he's about to strike, then duck, and come up under his shield arm, tipping him neatly to the grass. Then I stand aside, and wait for him to stand up.

This proves to be a mistake. On foot, he's better than I am.

Sometimes, I think altruism is not a survival characteristic. I wind up desperately trying to hold my guard against a flurry of fast and rather accurate attacks. Holy saints be thanked this is only for fun… I'm certain by now that whoever he is, he's not Andred. There's a suspicion building at the back of my mind… Parrying in quarte, I find I'm being backed almost into the other combat, and have to step aside hastily. The grass is wet. I keep my footing, but behind me, some-one curses, and goes down.

Abruptly, the serpent-rose is wide open. He's not even looking at me. Before I've quite finished debating whether it would be fair or not to hit him, he pushes past me.

There's an "Ouf" from behind me. Then Safere says, conversationally "You little bastard."

"He fell. Accidental advantage. You were going to follow up on it. That's not fair."

I know that voice… I turn, and start to fumble with my helm. The familiar voice goes on, "This was meant to be in fun!"

"Who for?" Safere sounds scornful. "Not, me, most certainly."

"You have no sense of honour…"

There's a pause, then Safere throws his shield to the ground and stalks away.

Kay has climbed to his feet. Wrenching open his visor, he glares at me. "You and your damned feuds."

"I'm sorry."

"Hrmph." Then he looks at the serpent-rose. The latter has raised his visor, and is looking at us in some irritation. "Lamorak de Galis. I might have known."

"Sir Kay!" Lamorak sounds embarrassed. He glances over his shoulder towards Safere's retreating back. "I thought…"

I've finally got my helm off. "I'm here," I say, apologetically. "We swapped."

"*You* fought me?"

"Well, yes."

"Deliberately?"

"No. Yes… Well, I didn't know who you were…"

"You *fought* me…"

"Saint Michael and all the archangels!" Kay has no time for amateur dramatics. "Gaheris had simply had enough of fighting your homicidal Moorish friend – and I'm beginning to see his point, too. If you didn't want to fight us, you should have said so; if you youngsters would stop changing your devices at the drop of a hat, this kind of muddle wouldn't happen. Lamorak stares at him, warily. "I'd say you owe Safere an apology."

"But he..." Lamorak looks at me, and stops. Then he bows, and goes across to Safere's tent.

Kay and I exchange glances. After a moment, he shakes his head, and says "Don't ask."

So I don't. About ten minutes later, Lamorak comes back, smiling, and invites us to stay the night and share their accommodation. I'm uncertain, but somehow I find myself cajoled into co-operation. Before I'm really ready to agree to it, I'm bathed, changed, and sitting in a nicely appointed pavilion drinking a wine that has been chilled to near perfection by the convenient river. The squires are pitching a third tent, and Kay is swimming.

Safere still seems to be sulking.

Lamorak is sprawled on a pile of cushions, looking Moorish enough himself. He's picked up a fine tan, and there's a new scar down his left forearm. He's wearing a ring that looks vaguely familiar.

"Well, you've certainly made yourselves comfortable."

"It *is* nice, isn't it? We get a fair amount of action, being on the road. And it's handy for... this and that."

My aunt Elaine has a castle not half a day's ride from here. Suddenly I've a context for the ring, too: what was it Gawain said about Mother's summer itinerary...?

"Oh, Lamorak. You're not still playing up to my mother?"

"I like her."

"So you said. But..."

"And your aunt has an excellent library. Safere..."

I don't want to hear Safere's opinions on books. "I think you should stop seeing her."

"Why?"

"Because…" I cast around for the right words. "Well, because your father may have killed mine – no, don't butt in – and my brother Gawain certainly killed your father, and…"

"Aglovale…"

"Be quiet. And because my mother isn't entirely… wholesome. She dabbles in things that aren't very healthy. *And…*" And I fix him with my best Gawain-style glare, "Most importantly, if they ever get to hear about it, my brothers Agravaine and Medraut would probably try to kill you."

"If they could."

"If they could. By foul means when fair failed. And if you were to kill one of them, you'd have Gawain to answer to, and he isn't a pushover. And after Gawain, Gareth and me."

"Would you care?"

"If you killed Gavin? Certainly."

"If he – or any of them – killed me."

"Of course I would. The last thing I want is the revival of that stupid feud."

Lamorak looks down. "The feud. That's all?"

"Don't fish." He swallows. "All right. Yes, I would mind if they killed you." He looks up, eyes shining. "I wish you'd be a little more sensible, that's all."

"I can't." he smiles. "It's in my family, you know. Aglovale got all that: the rest of us are unbalanced."

"Don't be ridiculous."

"No, I mean it. Percevale and I – and Dornar, too – we're none of us quite… normal."

"Tor was normal enough."

"Tor was only half a Pellinor. My parents were cousins, you know."

"My father was a homicidal maniac, and my mother's a witch. I don't think that makes *me* crazy."

"Ah, but you're like Aglovale." Lamorak looks at me oddly. "Everything about you has such clarity. Like flawless glass."

"Oh, aye. Completely transparent!" I laugh.

Lamorak starts to protest that he didn't mean it quite like that, but halfway through gives up and starts laughing too. And somehow I lose sight of persuading him to give up Mother.

Late that night, as I'm falling asleep, Kay says suddenly "Heris?"

"Umm?"

"I think you should stay away from Lamorak."

"Why? Because of Safere?"

He sighs, in the darkness. Then I hear him shrug. "No. Because of Lamorak."

Five

The rest of the year is normal enough. Tristan breaks the monotony somewhat by starting a new scandal: in between running for his life, he still finds time to discuss knightly rankings with all and sundry. He tells Gauter, who's an old Cornish gossip, that he'd place me in the top five, higher than any of my brothers. And Gauter tells Dinadan, who tells Ywain, who tells Gawain, who passes it on to me in high delight.

"I knew you had it in you. Don't say I never told you so."

"Oh, absolutely, Gavin."

Praise from Tristan is another good reason for avoiding knocking Cornish kings into the dust.

That Christmas, Medraut gets his knighthood, and heads out on his year's errantry. This would be nice and peaceful for the rest of us, only Mother elects to visit. About a month later, the king chooses a handful of new companions of the Round Table. This includes Lamorak, who's been hanging around court since late November, getting under my feet, and generally impeding the healing of his wrist, which Ector de Maris has kindly cracked for him. Luckily, Luned, forgiving his earlier gallantries, decides he reminds her of her brother, and finds plenty of occupation for him; winding wool and so forth.

Kay snorts darkly, but refuses to expand on his warning.

I can't see the harm in our friendship, though I do notice an odd look or so from Agravaine's friends. Not even Agrin actually says anything, however: injured or not, Lamorak has become a force to be respected.

It's a dark February evening when we all come together in the great hall, each companion in his own place, silent and with the tapers unlit before us. Only Lancelot, as champion, stands apart, ready to give and receive the three blows. White-clad, the candidates must pass him, and come before the king, to swear the oath and take the flame. After, they must circle the hall one by one, lighting the tapers of those assembled, and exchanging the kiss of peace. Taper by taper, until the whole room is a circle of fire.

That's my favourite bit. (That, and the dancing that follows, when the ladies come in.) The lights seem to leap from hand to hand, like a spirit, or an idea given life. Agravaine says I have it wrong, and that the whole is far more complex. But that's what I've seen since the first time, when I was the lighter of candles.

Anyhow, it takes different people different ways. Some are solemn as monks. Some are close to laughter. I mind our Gareth wept; and not the only one. Percevale fainted. And Gaheris? Gaheris of Orkney totally forgot the need for silence, and exclaimed "Oh, Gavin, look!", as he completed the circle at the king's left hand.

We're spared any excesses this time. Lamorak comes round the last of all; and as he rises from where the king has spoken to him, he looks round into the gloom, snake-eyes bright. He can't possibly see any of us properly, here in the darkness, but I smile anyway. Gareth beside me puts a hand on my arm.

That look to him... that shining quality... I'm thinking of Lancelot's words as Lamorak comes round us all, and I'm suddenly cold. To shine, he will have to live. On his hand that is illuminated, lighting the tapers, gleams my mother's ring. If Agravaine should notice, when Lamorak gets to him...

Little fool. There's such joy in his face, as he reaches me, that my heart stops still. He's too damnably young. My hands are shaking so much that I drop my taper, and have to fumble for it in the dark, fingers mixing with Lamorak's. We're forbidden to speak. I can do little about his confusion, as I tug the ring free, only frown. Lamorak looks into my eyes for an instant, then he's past me, and Gareth's taper is springing into life.

I'm in need of a drink. I'm profoundly thankful when the doors open and the rest of the court floods in. Gareth is looking at me curiously. "Are you all right, Heris?"

"What? Oh, yes. Hot wax." What if Agrin noticed...? I'm looking round for him, but there are too many people.

"Oh, that explains it, then." Gareth isn't really paying attention: he's trying to spot Llinos. "Better put something on it. Butter, isn't it, for burns?"

"I thought that was cats."

He turns. "For burns? Alive or dead?"

"No, no. Butter for cats. To stop them wandering." Some-one has put a full glass in front of me: I drain it gratefully. Lamorak is nowhere in sight, either, but I can see Percevale steering purposefully towards me. All this and now religion. "Gari?"

"Hmm?"

"Do something for me?"

"Of course." He's sighted Llinos, and was beginning to wave to her.

Now his courtesy takes over. "What?"

"Field Percevale for me? I'm not feeling up to it."

He looks down at me, then, concerned. "You do look pale. Shall I call Evan to you?"

"No, I'm just tired." He looks doubtful. "And lazy." He pulls a face. He's kind, Gareth. "Thanks, little brother."

He smiles. "You're welcome.

I don't find Lamorak, but after a couple of hours, I nearly walk into Safere, in a corner by the kitchen door. We've mostly avoided each other since the summer, and he doesn't look pleased to see me. I apologise, shuffling, then: "My lord Sir Safere?"

"What?"

"I was wondering if you... That is, Lamorak... "

"Yes?" He smiles at me nastily. He's rather drunk.

"I was looking for him."

"His heart will beat the faster for it."

"Yes, well, I wondered if you…"

"Little snake," says Safere, glittering with spite, "may be anywhere. Perhaps he is drowning his sorrows. He is too slight to withstand your disapprobation."

"I thought you might… What?"

He puts a hand on my shoulder, and leans on me. "Do you read Greek, Prince Gaheris?"

"No." I rather want to get away from him. He looks up at me from beneath his lashes. "Lamorak does…"

"Well, I expect he had a better tutor. But, really, Safere…"

"Do you want to know what he calls you?" He really is very drunk. I start to pull away, and he tightens his grip. "He talks about you all the time. In bed, even. Especially in bed."

"Let me go, please."

"I thought you wanted to know where little snake is laired? Beautiful Gaheris?"

"No. Not particularly. It can wait." His touch repels me. It takes much of my self-control not to push him away. "Please let go of me."

"His favourite topic. Beautiful Gaheris."

I don't want to hear this. For a slight man, he's surprisingly strong. If I have to force myself free, I may break his arm. He looks up at me, and begins to laugh. "I disgust you, don't I? The little sodomite. Alas, then, for Lamorak."

"I don't have any opinion of you."

"No? Why, then, do you shake so?"

I'm not shaking, I can't be shaking. "Claustrophobia." In this room full of people, surely someone will come to my aid. "I don't like dark corners."

"Or tight ones." Safere is still smiling. "Little snake has conceived an unholy passion for you. That's why he beds with your mother. "

"You're drunk." Oh, God, where's Agravaine.? If he's in earshot of any of this...

"Perhaps that is where he is even now. Substituting one Orkney for another."

I feel sick. Over Safere's shoulder, I can make out the broad silhouette of Gawain, the bright sheen of Gareth's hair. No Agravaine. No Lamorak. No Mother. Holy saints. Across the crowd, my eyes meet Lancelot's, and he looks puzzled. I can't afford to attract too much attention. Come on, Lance... Something in my face must speak to him, for he bows to his companions, and begins to make his way towards me. Now pray...

"Safere?"

"Yes, my dear lord prince?"

"Is that where Lamorak is? In my mother's room?"

"That is possible." He leans against me, loosening his grip. At last. I get my hand around his wrist, and twist. He gasps.

"Stop playing games. Where's Lamorak?"

"You are hurting me."

"For heaven's sake, Safere, this is important." Lancelot has nearly reached us. "Where is he? I swear to God, I'll break your arm."

Safere looks up, and all the haziness is gone from his eyes. "You astonish me. You really mean it, don't you?"

"Just try me."

"What in God's name...?" Lancelot has arrived, and is staring at us in some disbelief. "Gaheris, I don't think..."

"Where's my mother?" I ask him.

"What?" Lancelot frowns at me. "Are you all right, Safere?"

"He's fine. Where's the queen of Orkney?"

"I don't see..."

"Lancelot!"

"Very well." He looks at me as at a loose wolf. "She excused herself about an hour ago, feeling unwell."

Oh, God... Safere shifts a little, and I tighten my hold on him.

"And Agrin? My brother Agravaine?"

"Still talking to Bors and Bleobaris, as far as I know. What *is* this?"

"Does he know about Mother?"

"How should I know?"

"Think!"

"How much have you had to drink, Gaheris?"

"Less than you, almost certainly." He looks unconvinced. "Lancelot, this could be a matter of life and death. If Agrin hears that our mother is ill, he'll go to her room."

"So?" Lancelot looks at Safere, then back at me. "What is all this about?"

"Love." says Safere, sweetly, and smiles. "Or, perhaps, mere lust.

"What?"

"Charming Gaheris is perturbed over an *affajre de coeur*. He is trying to prevent a hypothetical murder. And all for the sake of a fine pair of yellow eyes."

I still can't see any sign of Agravaine. I may already be too late...

Lancelot folds his arms. "All right. Explain it to me very slowly. And, Gaheris?"

"Yes?"

"Let Safere go."

"But..."

"Just do it." Reluctantly, I release Safere's arm. He rubs it resentfully, but doesn't walk away. Lancelot continues, "Now, then?"

"It's Lamorak. He's been carrying on with my mother. I think he's up there with her now. And if Agravaine finds out, or goes up to see her, thinking she's ill... "

"I can imagine. A lover *and* a de Galis." Lancelot frowns. "Not very discreet of them. But I'm sure we can prevent Agravaine from surprising them, this time, at least."

"If he hasn't already done so."

"Calm down, Heris."

"But I haven't seen him all evening."

"He's over under the gallery, next to Bleobaris. He's been there for the last hour to my certain knowledge: I can still see him clearly. And I'm quite sure it's him."

Oh, thank you, God. I shall light three candles... "If you could make sure he stays down here for the next half hour or so, I'll deal with Lamorak and Mother."

"Is that wise?"

"You know my family."

"Well, I suppose so, but..."

"Forgive me; I intrude upon your deliberations, but..." Safere bows, smiling. There's something unpleasant about it. "Your precautions are admirably considerate, but quite unnecessary. Little snake is probably no longer with your mother."

"What?" I'm ready to hit him: Lancelot stays my hand. "You said that."

"I said that there was a possibility." Safere props himself on the wall. "For which you abused me quite outrageously."

I'm surprised no one's done it before... I have to stay calm. "Well, I'm sorry, then. But Lamorak..."

Safere shrugs. "Quite the centre of the world. Little snake *was* with your mother. But someone golden and perfect made a show of ritual disapproval earlier this evening, and tipped the balance of his indecisive mind. Little snake finally concluded it was in his long term interest to bid the sweet queen adieu."

"Lamorak went to break off his liaison with my mother?"

"That was what I said, yes."

"When? Where is he now?"

Safere studies his fingertips. "Desolated though I am, I must confess I have no idea. It is upwards of an hour since he left to perform the delicate deed."

Lancelot has been standing in apparent thought. Now he meets my eyes, and says, "I heard an odd story about your mother and Macsen of Rheged...?"

"It's true." My heart is racing. The room has turned cold.

Mother is a worse loser than Agrin… "Lancelot?"

"Yes?"

"Keep Agravaine down here. Gawain too, if possible. I'm going up."

"Wouldn't I be more… diplomatic?" Lancelot asks.

"This is an Orkney matter." Lancelot bows. I say, "Safer?"

"Beautiful Gaheris?"

"I know you don't like me, but for Lamorak's sake, get a horse saddled and waiting by the south gate, just in case…" For the first time, there's a flicker of concern on his face. I'm probably over-reacting, but my mother can be as blood-thirsty as the rest of my family, and she hates to be rejected.

It's hard, keeping to a walk as I make my way out of the hall, and once I'm through it, I give up and start to run. I take the stairs two at a time. The antechamber of my mother's room is completely deserted. Her door stands closed. No sounds come from behind it. There's a faint, sweet smell, like incense.

I don't knock. The door, mercifully, isn't locked. It opens quietly, at a touch.

Oh, sweet Jesu.

The candle-light is merciless. There's blood staining the rushes and the hangings of the bed. The coverlet is torn, and hangs mostly onto the floor. The air is heavy with blood and scent. Nothing looks quite real. Lamorak is crouched in the hearth, his arms wrapped tightly around him, His clothing is torn and stained. There's no sign at all of Mother. When I touch him, he pulls back as if burnt. There's a gash across his left cheek, and another along the line of his collar-bone. His eyes are unfocussed. He's trembling. I've seen men like this, after battle… The whole thing is like a distorted rerun of that night three years ago, when he asked me to knight him.

I have to find out what's happened here. I fetch water from the antechamber, and lock the door. He doesn't move.

"Lamorak?" When there's no answer, I take him by the shoulder, and shake gently. "Lamorak, wake up." He's limp in my hands. "Lamorak." I shake harder, and this time, he moans, pressing a hand to his side.

I pull it away. Well, that explains the blood. Oh, sweet Jesu. "Lamorak, talk to me." Holding on to him with one hand, I begin to wash the blood away. "Tell me what happened." His eyes are beginning to focus. I smile at him, and say gently, "You're safe, now. It's over. Just tell me what happened to you."

He licks his lips. "Gaheris."

"Who else?"

"Always sorting me out."

"Someone has to."

He smiles a little, at that. "Sorry."

"I know." My bathing hits a sensitive spot, and he winces. "What happened?"

The smile goes. "I tried to tell her it was over. After tonight…"

"The business with the ring. I understand."

"She…" He swallows. "Gaheris…"

"Still here."

"Yes. She cried, and I tried to… to comfort her. But she… there was a knife. She stabbed me."

The man who wrote that hell hath no fury was understating his case. He'd clearly never met Mother. Lamorak is shaking, and I put an arm around him. He clutches at me, gasping. "Slowly. It's over."

"No. Oh, Gaheris…"

"Not even the king's half-sister can get away with attempted murder. She won't hurt you again."

"You don't understand. Gaheris, I'm frightened."

"No need." I'll fix the others, somehow. He's been punished enough. And to hell with Safere.

"Gaheris."

"What is it?"

"Your brothers… "

"I'll deal with them."

"No." he pulls away suddenly. The snake eyes are wild. "You don't understand."

"What?"

He swallows again, hard, and points to the bed. "Under the quilt... I didn't mean..."

I can just about reach from here: I flick the coverlet aside with one hand, confused. Then everything stands still.

Oh, holy God.

It's Mother. She lies in a graceless heap. Her neck is bent the wrong way. I don't understand why, but suddenly I'm crying, and it's Lamorak who turns comforter. His hand catches mine. His fingers are cold. "Gaheris. My heart."

"Don't."

He leans away. "It was an accident. I swear to God. I only meant to push her away, but she lost her balance, and..."

"Yes." I swallow. "Perhaps she's only unconscious."

"No. I... checked."

"What a God-forsaken mess..." I rub a hand across my eyes, and start trying to think. "Who knew about you and Mother?"

"Several people. I... wore her favour in Cornwall."

"Tristan?"

"Yes."

Wonderful. He has all the discretion of a magpie. "We've got to get you away from here. Do you think you can ride?"

"Perhaps." He looks across at me. "Gaheris..."

"No, listen. My brothers would come after you for openly being her lover, let alone..." My throat is closed. I have to stop, to swallow, to regain control. "So I tell them I've already dealt with you. But you have to stay away."

"I don't understand. It was an accident."

"I believe you. Gareth would. Gawain might. But Agravaine and Medraut... They will try and kill you."

"As you warned me." His voice is bleak. "Do you know, I don't care. "

"Yes, you do. Just now; you're in shock. You have to protect yourself. You have to leave; now. Say you're on a quest, or a pilgrimage, or something. And, with luck, they'll never suspect you were here."

"But…" he glances across at the body, and turns pale.

"We have to explain the blood, too… Well, I have the Orkney temper. I expect I did it. Agrin would believe that, anyway. He never did like me much."

"What?" He's weeping, silently, without his old drama. "Gaheris, no. You can't. I won't let you."

"*Listen.*"

"They'll kill you instead."

"I'm one of them, Lamorak. Kin. Even Agrin respects that."

"But…"

"Can you think of anything better?"

"No… I can't think." He reaches out to me: I take his hand. "Why should anyone believe you?"

"Why not? A family quarrel – a tragic accident. We're famous for those, the Orkneys. And Mother has never been particularly fond of me."

"But…"

Oh, God. "Lamorak, think. This is a question of your life. Your life, or my honour. There's no contest."

"I can't let you do this."

"Why? Do you want to die?"

He stares at me in silence for long moments. Then he says "Yes. If that's the price of your name."

"Don't be ridiculous. This is no time for…"

He interrupts me. "I'm not. It's the one thing I could never tell you. How I feel about you."

"Lamorak, I…"

"No, you listen." Suddenly, he looks older. "I could never find a way to say it… I owe her that, at least." He looks at the body again, and shivers. "Gaheris – dear Gaheris – I don't know what you've made of me, all these years, but I don't think of you as my mentor, or my companion-at-arms, or even my hero. It's quite simple. I love you."

Safere said… It makes no sense. Not of me. It's on the tip of my tongue to deny it, but Lamorak shakes his head. "I mean it,

Heris. My Gaheris. I'm in love with you. I always have been. And I daresay you now despise me." The last word is almost inaudible: he looks down, and hides his face in his hands.

I get to my feet. There's a lot of people I love; my family, friends... No one I love in this sense, no one I love as Gawain did Rhanillt, as Lancelot loves... his lady. As Lamorak loves...

No.

I have to get him out of here. He's crying again, as if his heart is breaking. Agravaine will try to kill him if any of this gets out. I can at least give him a head start. I owe him that much.

I don't want to think about this. I have to explain the death, the blood... It's all his, there's not a mark on her. I have to explain the violence of it... His blood is on my clothing, too, and my hands, and I am whole. Why would she seek to stab *me?* What could I have done to her? Or she to me... The idea forms as I look again at Lamorak. Safere's word for himself, what was it... An insult to any man... All my family are crazy; my father was a maniac, and my mother's a witch...

Agravaine's no fool. If Lamorak stays here wounded, he'll put the pieces together. I go back to Lamorak, and put my hands on his shoulders. He won't look at me. "Can you stand?" No answer. "Listen, Lamorak; I don't despise you. I'm even quite fond of you. But right now, I'm trying to save your life, and you have to help me. Lean on me... that's it..."

Somehow I get him downstairs, and outside, to where Safere's waiting with two horses. Our eyes meet as we hoist Lamorak onto to one of them, and Safere says "I'm going with him."

"I'm glad." I say. "Take him a long way and keep him there."

"I will." He doesn't ask for details. I'm grateful for that.

Lamorak looks back at me as they start to move away, and his lips form my name. I shake my head at him, cautioning silence, and he looks down.

Then I go back to the tower, and I cut off my mother's head.

It doesn't work, of course. My mother's *affaire* with Lamorak is better renowned than I'd hoped; and too many people draw conclusions from his departure. Some go so far as to accuse him of the murder: one more act in our feuders' tragedy. And even those who happily credit me with the killing refuse to belief he's not involved in some way. The favoured story, in the end, has me finding them abed, and slaughtering Margawse in jealous outrage.

No one hazards any comments as to the object of my jealousy, in my hearing, at least. The king of necessity holds an enquiry: his jury of my peers acquit me, finally, complaining of inconclusive evidence. No death, no exile; only the enduring cloud of penance and suspicion. It seems that no one is willing to be quite sure. Sometimes, I catch my uncle watching me, and in his face are pity, and concern. Perhaps Lancelot has told him something. Perhaps he knows me more than I had thought.

I wish I was a better liar.

Not even Agravaine seems to think it worth the trouble of trying to kill me. He avoids me, muttering darkly about Lamorak; and corresponds with Medraut.

Kay stands by me. He doesn't even say, "I told you so."

I discover I'm missing Lamorak. There's no word of him for the longest time, although through Segwarides I learn that Safere, at least, is in Gaul. And after half a year or so, most people cease to speak of it.

Then a red-disguised knight shows up at the royal tourney at Surluse. He carries a blank shield, and keeps his visor down. It's a game Lancelot has played a hundred times, only Lancelot's here under his own arms. And Lancelot never wore one of my gloves pinned to his shoulder as a token. Perhaps even with that, he might have got away with it, only Medraut recognises his squire. And then again, perhaps he was expecting it. I have no way of knowing. I know only that my brothers, having once located him, will not readily let him go. Not even Gawain, though he at least speaks of fair combat, and even of royal arbitration.

Nothing I say can change it. The knowledge, the bitterness, is fixed. Lamorak de Galis dishonoured our mother. Lamorak de Galis forced Gaheris" hand. Lamorak de Galis must pay.

I don't even get a chance to warn him: Agravaine dogs my every step. Lamorak leaves the tourney with the prize in his hand, and a price on his head. He leaves quite alone.

It's as though he's courting his death.

Gawain wakes me at dawn, the day after. "Agravaine's for following Lamorak. You must come, Heris."

"I can't."

"Aye. But you must, all the same."

"No... Can't you let it be? Leave him alone?"

"Perhaps I could. But Agrin, now, and Medraut... That's why you must come. To see it done fairly."

"Gavin, I can't."

His face is kind. "You're not understanding me. Agrin blames you, as well as Lamorak. If you don't come willing, he's for tying you, and bringing you perforce."

"Gavin... "

"Will you swear to me, on your oath of knight-hood, that Lamorak had no part in our mother's death?"

"That's not fair."

He puts a hand on my shoulder. "Can you swear it?"

Her fault, not his... "Will you let him be, and make sure Agrin and Medraut do, too?" He looks down. "Why, Gavin?"

"Happen it's the only way they can admit they loved her."

"And you?"

He sighs." I am the Eldest." He knows it's no answer. There are none, except the old tangle of Orkney pride. Orkney folly. "But you must come."

"I can't hurt him."

"Aye."

"And I don't think I can watch."

"You must."

I dress, arm myself, and mount in silence. In silence I ride, alongside Gawain, into the forest of Surluse. Don't look at Agrin.

Don't listen. Don't think.

I have never known a deeper shame. I cannot bear myself. I cannot bring myself to understand. I cannot even, any longer, hope.

Safere is safely in Gaul. Lamorak must have escaped him and run mad, to come back here.

He hasn't even tried to run. We find him in a wide clearing some eight miles from Surluse, pavilion pitching in plain sight, serpent-rose flying. He waits before it, fully-armoured save for his helm. As we ride in, he scans us anxiously. Then he sees me, and his face clears. He smiles. I meet his gaze, but cannot hold it for more than a moment. If I were a better man, a stronger one, we would never have come to this.

Gawain rides forward, and salutes him. "I must challenge you. Will you accept?"

"I will."

"Aye. Well, then…" Gawain sighs. "We'll fight here. But only you and me. And whichever wins, may give or refuse mercy as he will; and whatever happens then, that's an end to it, on my honour. No reprisals. Do you agree?"

"Willingly."

Gawain glares at Agravaine and Medraut. "Do you mind me? I will not have you breaking my word."

"As ever, Gavin." Agravaine says. Medraut simply bows. I can't speak. My eyes are locked on Lamorak. He's so calm. He seems so much older.

The squires help them ready themselves. My hands are damp on my reins. I can't bear this. The hoof-beats on the turf are like thunder, like battle drums. I can't watch the cut and thrust of sword blows. Lamorak is better than Gavin.

Gavin is my brother.

I'm not watching. I tell myself that, over and over. I am not looking at Medraut as he circles behind Lamorak, a crossbow in his hands. Agravaine seizes my arm, a knife in his hand to ensure I don't shout out a warning. I call out anyway, and my voice is lost in the volley of blows. Medraut's hands are white on the trigger. The bolt is silent as it arcs through the air. I press forward and Agrin's knife is a scarlet pain across my forearm. Time stops.

Then I'm on my knees on the grass, and my hands are bloody, and my face is wet. Lamorak has dragged his helm off, and is lying half against me. We've been here before, but this time there's death in it. Blood trickles from the corner of his mouth, as he tries to speak to me. Somewhere, some world away, I can hear Agravaine laughing.

"Beautiful Gaheris..." There's a smile for me, though the snake eyes are already dimming. I still can't speak. My hand finds his, and grips it, tightly. There's no answering pressure.

I'm sorry.

"Well," says Agrin, sweetly, "And how do you feel now about murdering Mother?"

Nothing. I feel nothing. Gavin says roughly "Be silent, Agrin, or I'll make you."

I look up, at Agrin, at Medraut. "You'll never live this down. Gavin had given his word."

"Aye," says Gawain, and his voice now is smooth as silk. "You swore to me. It was to be a fair fight."

"You might," says Medraut, silkily, "have lost."

"What of it? You've shamed me. This is a bad day's work. This taints us all forever." Gawain turns his back and stalks away. I have heard that that tone from him only once before in my life, and then it was death for anyone who came in his way.

Medraut just shrugs. He was still a child when Rhanillt died and Gawain lost his centre. Agravaine smiles, and rests a hand on my shoulder. "You see, Heris? You should have let me kill him all those years ago."

I push him away, leaving bloody marks on his surcoat with my bloody hands. "I wish you'd tried. Perhaps he'd have killed *you*. Because, God help me, I can't, and I wish I could."

Not even Gawain tries to stop me, as I mount up and ride away. Nor does he speak up that evening, when in front of all I take up my sword, and lay it at the feet of Aglovale de Galis.

Coda

High on a tower, high on a hill, two men are standing. One is square-built, iron-haired, solidly mature. The other, the younger, is made imposing only by his height. His countenance is unremarkable. The most common expression in his eyes is puzzlement. They wear that aspect now, puzzled; and a little sad, as they gaze out beyond the battlements, out into the mist, and the distance. He's the air of a bit- player, an extra, one who has no need to understand the lines, the acts, that fall to him.

Perhaps that's for the best.

The elder, the remarkable, is watching his face. His own is unreadable. In a quiet voice, he says, now, "I remember a squire, once, who contradicted his king, and rightly. Do you mind it?"

"I do, sire."

"There are two good knights lost for the sake of one. What changed, Heris?"

"I don't know, sire. Uncle. Perhaps I never really said it. Perhaps it just grew in the telling."

"You will leave yourself with nothing." The king puts his elbows on the parapet, and gazes out at his land. "We all will, if we turn on ourselves from within."

"You have other knights. Better knights than me."

"I have many unique men. I did not seat you all at a round table to be quantified by some external scale of ability." His voice drops. "Have I lost two more good knights, Gaheris, for the sake of one vain woman?"

"You have already lost one."

"Yes. Poor Lamorak."

"He came to die so gently. As though he wanted it."

"Yes. Poor Gaheris, too." The king is pensive. "What will you do now? Will you leave us?"

"I don't know. It shall be as you wish it, sire."

"Will it?" The king sighs. "Will you forgive your brothers, and forget the past, for the sake of one aging man?"

"No, sire." From the tower, one may see five counties, if the day is clear. "But I will do it anyway."

"Why, then, Gaheris?"

I turn my back to the wall. "Because Agrin would like it so, if I didn't."

Across five counties, the rain starts to fall.

About the Author

Kari Sperring is the author of *Living with Ghosts* (DAW 2009), (winner of the 2010 Sydney J Bounds Award, shortlisted for the William L Crawford Award and a Tiptree Award Honours' List book) and *The Grass King's Concubine* (DAW 2012). As Kari Maund, she's an academic mediaeval historian, and author of 5 books and many articles on early Welsh, Irish and Scandinavian history. With Phil Nanson, she is co-author of *The Four Musketeers: the true story of d'Artagnan, Porthos, Aramis and Athos*. She's British and lives in Cambridge, England, with her partner Phil and three very determined cats, who guarantee that everything she writes will have been thoroughly sat upon.

Her website is http://www.karisperring.com and you can also find her on Facebook.

More New Titles from NewCon Press

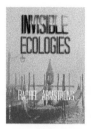

Rachel Armstrong – Invisible Ecologies
The story of Po, an ambiguously gendered boy who shares an intimate connection with a nascent sentience emerging within the Po delta: the bioregion upon which the city of Venice is founded. Carried by the world's oceans, the pair embark on a series of extraordinary adventures and, as Po starts school, stumble upon the Mayor's drastic plans to modernise the city and reshape the future of the lagoon and its people.

Kim Lakin-Smith – Rise
Charged with crimes against the state, Kali Titian (pilot, soldier, and engineer), is sentenced to Erbärmlich prison camp, where few survive for long. Here she encounters Mohab, the Speaker's son, and uncovers two ancient energy sources, which may just bring redemption to an oppressed people. The author of *Cyber Circus* returns with a dazzling tale of courage against the odds and the power of hope.

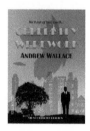

Andrew Wallace – Celebrity Werewolf
Suave, sophisticated, erudite and charming, Gig Danvers seems too good to be true. Appearing from nowhere, he champions humanitarian causes and revolutionises science,developing the first organic computer to exceed silicon capacity; but are his critics right to be cautious? Is there a darker side to this enigmatic benefactor, one that is more in keeping with his status as the Cleberity Werewolf?

Legends 3 – edited by Ian Whates
David Gemmell passed away in 2006, leaving behind a legacy of memorable characters, and thrilling tales. The *Legends* series of anthologies, of which this the third and almost certainly final volume, is intended to pay homage to one of fantasy fiction's greatest writers. Features a selection of dazzling stories written especially for the books by some of the finest fantasy authors around.

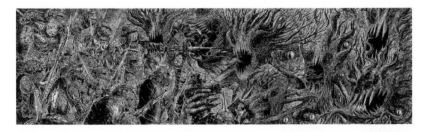

NewCon Press Novella Set 6: Blood and Blade

Four stand-alone novellas of sword play, sorcery, blood-drenched battles, noble deeds and fool-hardy endeavours, linked only by their shared cover art. Released summer 2019, in paperback, limited edition hardback, and as a slipcased set featuring all four novellas as signed hardbacks and **Duncan Kay**'s combined artwork as a wrap-around.

In **Edward Cox**'s *The Bone Shaker,* Sir Vladisal and her knights are lost within endless woodlands. Harried by demons, they seek the kidnapped son of their Duchess, facing terror at every turn. **Gaie Sebold** takes us on *A Hazardous Engagement,* wherein a wily gang of thieves are set an impossible task. Fortunately, they never know when to quit. In

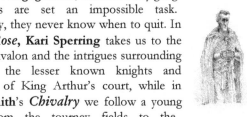

Serpent Rose, **Kari Sperring** takes us to the realm of Avalon and the intrigues surrounding some of the lesser known knights and characters of King Arthur's court, while in **Gavin Smith**'s *Chivalry* we follow a young knight from the tourney fields to the battlefield, where he is forced to grow up rapidly as he faces challenges beyond his wildest imaginings.

Four stunning tales of epic fantasy scaled down to novella size by four outstanding authors.

IMMANION PRESS
Purveyors of Speculative Fiction

Strindberg's Ghost Sonata & Other Uncollected Tales by Tanith Lee

This book is the first of three anthologies to be published by Immanion Press that will showcase some of Tanith Lee's most sought-after tales. Spanning the genres of horror and fantasy, upon vivid and mysterious worlds, the book includes a story that has never been published before – 'Iron City' – as well as two tales set in the Flat Earth mythos; 'The Pain of Glass' and 'The Origin of Snow', the latter of which only ever appeared briefly on the author's web site. This collection presents a jewel casket of twenty stories, and even to the most avid fan of Tanith Lee will contain gems they've not read before. ISBN 978-1-912815-00-5, £12.99, $18.99 pbk

A Raven Bound with Lilies by Storm Constantine

The Wraeththu have captivated readers for three decades. This anthology of 15 tales collects all the published Wraeththu short stories into one volume, and also includes extra material, including the author's first explorations of the androgynous race. The tales range from the 'creation story' *Paragenesis*, through the bloody, brutal rise of the earliest tribes, and on into a future, where strange mutations are starting to emerge from hidden corners of the earth. ISBN: 978-1-907737-80-0 £11.99, $15.50 pbk

The Lord of the Looking Glass by Fiona McGavin

The author has an extraordinary talent for taking genre tropes and turning them around into something completely new, playing deftly with topsy-turvy relationships between supernatural creatures and people of the real world. 'Post Garden Centre Blues' reveals an unusual relationship between taker and taken in a twist of the changeling myth. 'A Tale from the End of the World' takes the reader into her developing mythos of a post-apocalyptic world, which is bizarre, Gothic and steampunk all at once. 'Magpie' features a girl scavenging from the dead on a battlefield, whose callous greed invokes a dire curse. Following in the tradition of exemplary short story writers like Tanith Lee and Liz Williams, Fiona has a vivid style of writing that brings intriguing new visions to fantasy, horror and science fiction. ISBN: 978-1-907737-99-2, £11.99, $17.50 pbk

www.immanion-press.com
info@immanion-press.com